W9-ATT-096

REEL

Tobias Carroll

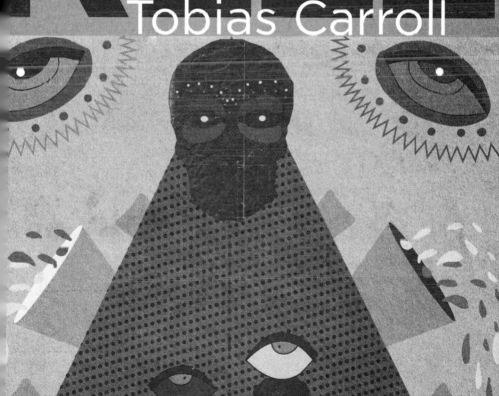

A BARNACLE BOOK • RARE BIRD BOOKS
LOS ANGELES, CALIF.

REEL

Tobias Carroll

THIS IS A GENUINE BARNACLE BOOK

A Barnacle Book | Rare Bird Books
453 South Spring Street, Suite 302
Los Angeles, CA 90013
rarebirdbooks.com

Copyright © 2016 by Tobias Carroll

FIRST TRADE PAPERBACK ORIGINAL EDITION

All rights reserved, including the right to reproduce this book or
portions thereof in any form whatsoever, including but not limited
to print, audio, and electronic. For more information, address: A
Barnacle Book | Rare Bird Books Subsidiary Rights Department, 453
South Spring Street, Suite 302,
Los Angeles, CA 90013.

Set in Minion Pro
Printed in the United States

Cover illustration by Ameu

10 9 8 7 6 5 4 3 2 1

Publisher's Cataloging-in-Publication data

Names: Carroll, Tobias, author.
Title: Reel , a novel / Tobias Carroll.
Description: First Trade Paperback Original Edition | A Barnacle
Book | New York, NY; Los Angeles, CA: Rare Bird Books, 2016.
Identifiers: ISBN 978-1-942600-70-1
Subjects: LCSH Punk culture—Fiction. | Punk rock music—Fiction. |
Friendship—Fiction. | Art—Fiction. | BISAC FICTION/General.
Classification: LCC PS3603.A7749 R44 2016| DDC 813.6—dc23

PART ONE:

ICONS

1

Timon met Marianne at a Black Halos show in Seattle. It wasn't the cold season yet, but its arrival loomed. Jackets and a few bold scarves could be seen on bodies on the streets surrounding the club. These were melancholy hours, a time to have impractical thoughts and ponder ways in and out on walks through the city.

The second opener had ended and the headliners had begun arranging their gear across the stage. Illumination was enough to see one's neighbor, be they acquaintance or stranger, but was not yet the clarifying light that signified the end of the night's music and stifled hopes of an encore. Through speakers came the sound of guitars wrapped around one another, a sinuousness evoked through unfamiliar rhythms. Seated at a table halfway between speakers and bar, Marianne wished for a change, for whoever handled such things to make a change, however abrupt the transition. She had hoped for something cerebral, some sort of literate pop, songs with lyrics she could run through her mind to trigger evocation. Instead: complex textures and low-slung fissures, atonal voices shouting in the distance.

Timon waited closer to the stage, beer in hand, poised like a soldier or skydiver.

She was there alone and he was there alone; she had come for the first opener, and he was there for no apparent reason, had been out on a walk, had seen that there was a show happening with tickets available as he passed by the club, and so he had forayed inside and ordered beer after beer after beer to pass the time. He had walked there down one hill and up another, and anticipated a brutal traversal of those same inclines on his homeward route. Timon wondered whether this might be the night he slipped and would be able to confirm his own theory of the downward roll, whether he would tumble until he reached a certain point in the sidewalk or instead overrun the curb and come to a terminal point mid-lane, either to raise himself up and begin his trek once more or to encounter vehicle, for rolling inebriated flesh colliding with decelerating but nonetheless lethal rubber and metal. And so Timon drank and awaited the headliner's arrival on the stage and, across the room, Marianne stood, feeling compelled to stay for more.

And when the band entered, garage-rock from across the state's northern border, Timon took a long drink from the bottle he'd been nursing for the past few minutes and thought of the phrases that had occupied his head for months. His grandfather's final words, relayed to him across a continent via his parents: "It's the fear," the phrase coming to Timon secondhand. "The fear." And that phrase dovetailing, curling around the title of the album that had occupied much of his stereo's time recently: I Am That Great and Fiery Force. And Timon thought, Yes: I will be that fear, and I will be that great and fiery force, and as the guitars began to roar he rushed into the crowd a dervish, eyes wide, seeking the contact of body on body, not willing destruction but not willing to prevent destruction, and so the spins, the loose arm, the images from the periphery of his vision of forms pushing backward, retreating from him. Retreating from no others, none yet joining him in this cleared space.

Timon thought of the fraying then, of the days as a child when he'd first been in adult spaces, spaces that had not seen anyone of his age in decades. His parents would be in another room, discussing arcane subjects with the building's occupants or caretakers. He would be left somewhere to wait, dressed in a style that mortified: an awkwardly patterned tie and a nondescript blue blazer, always a size too large. He would wait and while waiting he would simply observe. He began to catalog the accumulation of dust in certain houses and apartments and the lack of dust in others, the presence or absence of plastic covers for furniture, the ways in which window side drapes began to unwind, the manner in which certain colors faded from photographs taken in a certain decade.

As his parents would go about the family's business, he would begin his interrogation of the less-forthcoming photographs, trying to guess as best he could when they were taken. Trying to suppose the period, then the decade, then the specific year. And after he'd done this alone and in isolation for ten months, he finally posed his first question to the home's owner and learned that his estimate had been only two years off: 1926 rather than 1924. His parents nodded, never specifically encouraging him in this but never interjecting as he began to ask questions of each of their hosts, and began to formulate courses of study. And after another year, when his guesses as to the years had become encyclopedic in their accuracy, he turned his attention to location and time: Chicago on a cloudy day; a bright morning in Vilnius; a late-night reverie in Halifax, just after the end of the Great War.

In the club in Seattle, Timon swung out again and again, hands moving through the air. As he drove backward, his body encountered the hands of others, those hands pushing him back into the center of the room, into his emptied center, and he clenched and unclenched and nursed at his beer and began the process again. It was deeper each time, a constant kind of motion, obeying the dictates of the rhythm coming from the stage and the speakers, his mind empty as long as he could keep from stopping.

And from twenty feet away, Marianne's eyes drifted from the stage to the spinning, shaking figure to her left, and she thought, Christ, who is this asshole? Thought: this brutalist, making a fool of himself, wasted and stumbling. Thought: fucking imbecile, and edged herself further away from him. Over the sound of torn guitars her mind shifted to other topics: forgotten garage bands from steel towns and pulp novels and the lurid taste of drinks assembled by a bartender she'd once encountered in west Texas, on the drive that had brought her to Seattle several years before. There was a construction she had in mind, a loose collage of images from atlases documenting an impossible geography. It was a notion that had circulated and inspired her when she first came to this city, during a time when she had sought work and disciplines to occupy her time and delay the onset of panic. Soon after she had begun her sketches of the piece, steady work had arrived, and she had shelved the project. More recently, the notion of completing it had returned to her, along with the notion that its construction would return to her a kind of freedom of movement, would unbind her from the city in which she dwelt. A sort of thesis, then, or the end of a journeyman phase. She considered leaving the city more frequently now than she ever had before. As her eyes returned to the drunkard, she thought, And this will be the reason for my departure.

Eight songs in, Timon was still careening from body to body, was down to his last sips of the bottle, was earning the enmity of those around him, their faces shifting over time from acknowledgment to condemnation. Epithets and epitaphs hovered on low frequencies and Timon shifted in and out, hearing only sufficient syllables to comprehend the general mood of his vicinity. He continued to contort until something in his stomach wrenched and his face felt cold and his throat ran bilious, and he was off, pushing away from the stage, pushing through a section of the crowd unaccustomed to being pushed through.

Minutes later, he stood over the sink, hands cupped to drink. Cue the inspection: was it visible on him? Was he marked? He was not. And so he returned to the crowd, positioning himself toward the back now, assuming the rest of the set with arms at his sides, breathing easily, his stomach still allowing for telltale twinges but overall settled. He stood there as the band played their final song, stood there as the crowd began filing toward the club's exit.

Marianne was set to meet friends at a bar nearby to have a drink or two before closing. She looked down at her phone to check the time and joined the dwindling group walking outside. As she neared the bar, she saw the man she'd previously shunned. Now, he looked preternaturally still, like a monument or mile marker or memorial, his skin pale and his cheeks flushed, his eyes bloodshot. She looked at him, their eyes level. "Look, you," she began, and his attention flared up, his eyes met hers. "That's not okay, what I saw there. You keep doing that, people will deem you loathsome."

Timon swallowed, half expecting this to be a critique made in transit. She wasn't moving, though; she was standing there, looking him in the eye. Daring him, in Timon's mind, to say something. And standing there in an emptying club, the night's energy moved elsewhere, diminished by alcohol and the damages it had already wrought on his body, he could only think to absolve himself. "Meant nothing by it," he said, hoping that this simple phrase might lend him some humanity in her eyes, might convince her that he was not simply the blind thug he assumed she took him for; that he meant no harm in his unrestricted motion. He heard his words fall to the club's floor and realized that he sounded robotic, and he tried to hold the look of the woman opposite him. It was a conversation that was destined to fail, he realized.

He reached for his wallet and withdrew his business card. He handed it to her. "Here," he said tenderly, as though displaying a photograph of a newborn child. Then he said something like, "Damages." She held up one hand, palm facing him, and shook her head. Marianne stepped outside, making her way toward her friends. Timon waited at the bar and wondered whether he should order his night's final drink.

2

TIMON WAS THE WESTERN outpost of the family business. He rose late, hovering on a bridge shift, sometimes handling the family's clients on the Pacific coast and sometimes, as the sky grew dark, making terse conversation with early risers on that ocean's other shores. Sometimes he would cloak himself in respectable attire and drive far from the city to confer via video with the remainders of the firm: his father, now almost an academic with a small cabin in Princeton; his uncle Clark, gone reclusive on the coast of Baja California; his uncle Gilbert, newly settled in Istanbul; his cousin Kiasma, reluctantly listening from a space on the outskirts of Beijing. Which, Timon suspected, was not unlike the company's Seattle office: a dedicated room in an apartment or townhouse, its decor neutral, its tone wind-swept granite relative to the clamor around it.

During the slivers of time when Timon had been social, he had been pressed with questions about the family business and his seeming ambivalence toward it. The company had been a crucial piece of his parents' courtship; the business had provided a fulcrum around which they could interact, and it was to the despair of several generations of Timon's family that, following the marriage, his mother had opted to follow an academic career. "Looking back on it now, I could never have done it," she told him once during a fleeting trip he had made to the eastern seaboard. "Did you know that at the time," he asked her, knowing it to be an unfair question, a question lacking an answer, but feeling that it needed to be said. Or worse, that it was the question that should have been said, that he was simply the vessel for a selection of prepackaged words, of halves of hundreds of conversations that he need only stand in place to deliver.

His mother had shaken her head. "I couldn't tell you. I feel wholly divorced from who I was then. It's as though I'm reading a novelization of my own life story: the names and events ring true, but the motivations lack any sense to me now. I see a love story, but it's not mine."

When considering his parents' marriage, now nearing the thirty-year mark, Timon often wondered what lessons he might learn, what patterns he might emulate in his own life. This normally occurred prior to long sessions with whiskey, with thrice-distilled vodka, with stouts as dense as masonry. Sometimes there were calls back to his homestead: lurches and requests for forgiveness that encountered confused ears.

A city-boy friend of Marianne's had inevitably led to her coining the term "brunching econo." This had been years before, during the Omaha years; the term had stuck, however, and she had carried it with her to Seattle and used it to fuel the groups with which she ran. One of them had turned to her and said, "Does this mean we've just sold out punk rock?" And Marianne had laughed and said something charming, then let it slip her mind; then remembered it again and felt its memory issue regret that ran through her, a prompt for contortions and sudden glances toward rooms' empty corners and solitary figures, words issued in mid-air with no expected response.

Marianne and her friend Elias had driven north on an inexplicable day trip to Anacortes, the spiraled result of brunchtime discussion and the realization that neither of them had anything worth doing on the Sunday in question. Elias was a few years older than Marianne and had left the early part of his twenties swathed in denials and carefully parceled information. He had alluded to tattoos that no one should ever see, and in doing so had divulged one halfway-relevant piece of information at a party. "Ah," some drunkard had said, a rictus grin on his face. "You're an old fascist, then. Hate tattoos and National Socialist brands all across your arms."

Elias's face had gone pale, then red. He swallowed up torrents of anger that Marianne didn't believe him capable of possessing, then leaned in, his voice suddenly coarse.

"I sure as shit," he said, "would fucking quiet that shit down." His hands went to fists. "I sure as shit would not say one damned lie about me being a fascist." He turned his face up; the drunkard had four inches and thirty pounds on Elias, but it was his turn to go pale. "Do you comprehend? Call me a fascist, call me a racist, and things will break." And Elias looked up at the drunkard and waited for him to back away. Which, of course, he did.

On the road to Anacortes, the subject of Elias's tattoos was raised once more. "There's a rumor floating around," said Marianne, "that the reason you came to Seattle was for the climate. That you wouldn't ever need to wear short sleeves, that it wouldn't look unnatural." There was silence from Elias, and Marianne paused, unnerved, feeling a sudden fear that Elias might whip his car around and return them to Seattle, or would simply leave her stranded roadside. Instead, Elias emanated something that looked distinctly like a smile.

"You've known me two years," he said. "You've seen me in ninety, ninety-plus weather. You ever know me to sweat?" She smiled, then shook her head. Elias was one of those peculiarly blessed people with taut frames who rarely, if ever, perspired. "I'm a kind of freak, but it's a convenient sort of freakishness. That said, I don't know that I could have pulled off this particular look, this particular style, somewhere else. As much as I suspect that I'm a man destined for the desert somewhere, Arizona or Albuquerque was not to be my home."

"Then why Seattle?" Marianne asked.

Elias shook his head. "1 had reasons, you know. And I still do."

They stopped thirty miles north of the city for coffee; it was the sort of trip that was as much about stimulants on the journey as it was about the destination itself. Elias was a notoriously inefficient driver in this way, and as such his trips were prized by those that accompanied him.

They stepped out of the car at a small roadside kiosk that friends had recommended after a similar trip two months earlier. It appeared to be a prefab shed that had been modified in some essential and unsettling way, its walls and roof lengthened, an asymmetric window carved into one side for the taking and distribution of orders. It was as though someone or some group had done their best to remake the space, as generic a structure as one could envision, as something organic, something fully formed and uniquely conceived, something withdrawn from a womb. And as they parked out front and approached it, they saw the mural, the work of an artist they knew from Seattle by style if not by name. The thought entered Marianne's mind seemingly from nowhere: that this artist would not be out of place in Europe, that his or her linework and sense of form and placement of bodies aligned more closely with images she had seen of street art an ocean away than with the forms that alighted on buildings and infrastructure in the spaces with which she was familiar.

Around the structure, four bodies, just under life-sized, had been painted. Three men, one woman, each somewhat stylized, each making some sort of offering. It was highly symbolic, Marianne thought: there was a quality of the religious to it, as though it could have adorned, with few alterations, the center of a stained-glass window or the walls of a Mayan temple.

The figures looked dressed for a funeral, Marianne thought: the men wore black suits, and the woman a long black dress. The first of the men held out a heart; the second, a knife. Marianne stared at the textures and ventured a guess as to the type of paint used, and after some consideration, decided that she was not feeling particularly optimistic about the level of symbolism on display. The third figure was the woman. She was holding something up, further from her body than the other figures; upon closer inspection, Marianne recognized the object as a loose strand of film. The fourth figure held a playing card in one hand, and covered his mouth with the other. Strange, thought Marianne, and then paused from turning away from the mural. The height of the figure, the look in his eyes—it looked not unlike the man she had reprimanded some time ago.

She looked around the mural for some indication of when it had been made, and perhaps for a trace of information on the artist. A lost cause, she assumed, but one worth pursuing. After completing a full circuit of the structure, she saw no signature, but did see a scrawl that resembled a date closely enough that she saw fit to deem it as such. It was close enough to the present day that the drunkard could very well have been the model for the figure in question. Marianne shook her head to herself, eliciting a brief exhalation from Elias. "Forensic scene done?" he said, bearing coffee-rooted drinks in his hand.

"Give me just a second," she replied, and wandered to the kiosk's window, making inquiries about the mural. The recipient of those questions shrugged. "I started here last week," they said. "Can't tell you much about it." Marianne thanked them and took her beverage; with Elias, she ventured back to the car. They continued north to Anacortes, where music and revelry awaited.

3

Timon's Monday began with a slash of daylight across his face, one eye's view rendered red through still-shuttered lids. A silent, monolithic awakening, and his attempts to stir it away. His body felt knotted as he contracted his knees, pivoted, and readied himself to stand. A root between his shoulders tightened, loosened, then tightened again as though maintaining its own rhythms. He palmed one alarm and looked at it. Seven in the morning. An awakening with the dawn, then. Still, ten back at the home office, and a verification due this day. Timon to the shower, cold water on his face to accelerate waking, though not to abate the aches that ran through him like finely tethered circuitry.

Static in the upper arms, suffusing his triceps with a perpetual dwindling. Mornings like these, he would feel it and in paranoid times wonder if this was the onset of a heart attack, if it was some revenant prefiguring agitation and horror before collapse. Two keloid scars behind his shoulders danced a chrysalis twist. Sometimes the ache would drift into his legs, idle, then swiftly dissipate. He felt the pattern of his day's discomfort emerge, felt a desire to reshape himself.

His sister had advised him to jog on mornings such as these. "You'll get the demons out," she said. Timon considered it, saw her wisdom, and yet. Not this morning, he told himself—the early beginning seemed progress enough.

The walls of his apartment stood slate-gray, windows' light slapping Modernist designs across them at odd angles, yielding curious framings. The walls stood unadorned, their color in some cases obstructed by a standardized series of black bookshelves. Books on art, on history. Monographs, cultural dictionaries, museum catalogs— some his own and some given to him for the business, to act as reference or reminder of facts that had enveloped him at an early age, the phrase "formative years" feeling all too literal on the rare occasions when he encountered it.

At the end of the room stood a desk. The sleeping area was sectioned off from the work area with a series of screens; the bathroom door stood next to his workspace, an awkward location tolerated only because it allowed his desk a placement below his street-view window, sometimes his only indication of the day's progression and measure. There were days when he would descend into dimly lit rooms on dark mornings and emerge into darkened evenings and feel a dislocation, a removal from thc days and weeks of others; an exemption from the cycles experienced by those around him.

He had once had a routine in this city that was considered normal, albeit briefly. It had cycled him out, though—his timing never entirely lining up with that of the people around him, and so he had considered himself dispatched, whether or not he had actually faced that verdict.

This particular morning began with a message from his father—a project undertaken for Yannick Sarja, a longtime client.

Timon's family was in the business of verification. They were consultants, of a sort—hired by clients, generally individuals rather than institutions, to delve into the history of notable objects, to ascertain whether certain suppositions about them were, or were not, accurate. They dwelled in a world of artifacts rather than one of fine art; they did not sniff out forgeries or subject paint-shrouded canvases to chemical and X-ray analyses. Timon understood that there was some precedent for this; an uncle of his had taken on a few assignments of this nature, but that the firm's founder, Timon's grandfather, had discouraged it. "That's for others," Timon, at twenty, had heard him say. "Our work lies in the artisanal, in things forged and manufactured. Leave art to the scientists and critics."

And so they had.

Timon took breakfast at a corner café two blocks east. Took cheese on a croissant and called himself sated; walked out the door, still sipping coffee, face turned away from the wind that darted through his hair like downhill racers passing snow-leavened gates. He felt a slow-motion revival spread through his body, a Pentecostal elation returning certain tissues to a joyful baseline. Six blocks toward the interstate was the address at which he maintained a mailbox, and he walked there now, wondering if the coffee would expire before the distance did.

Timon's grandfather had built the firm, in its early days. His sons had been raised into it—the notion that the business was everything, could become anything. When he considered it, considered the disciplines pursued by his father and his uncles, he wondered how much coaxing it had taken on his grandfather's part, and how much steering. Had they reduced pursuits out of passion, or from it?

His father and uncles had briefly been fast-track academics, polymaths in an increasingly specialized world. Their line of work, then, seemed oddly fitting. The arrival of Timon's generation had prompted a new system, upon which two generations had convened in order to develop. Timon himself had known little of it as he grew up—it was simply his default mode, a constant barrage of facts and stimuli, amniotic knowledge, constant renewal; associations, constantly formed. A mind honed for verification and drawn toward the obscure. He had, ironically, learned more about his own rearing when researching, in one spell of downtimes, certain educational theories of the twentieth century, some now considered heretical or apocryphal. These were moments in history, systems of thought, that Timon would find cross-referenced in his own research. The balance, at his father's urging—three-quarters for the firm, one-quarter for himself. And so Timon's quarter was spent hovering around documents of cultural subcultures, monographs of punk photography, and underground semiotics. And, on certain evenings, the pursuit of guitars distorted or fuzzed out, of snare and bass hard-hit in small rooms, lightning rounds, and whiskey shots. Timon's promise to himself of neutrality on just one occasion: a vow, constantly snapped. And in the morning, regrets.

He came to rest at the mailbox. There he received a handful of envelopes, as well as one box for which he was required to sign. Its construction was a masterpiece of trim symmetrical security, thick tape lashed around and across cardboard. While Timon could place its outline, could recognize intellectually that the object before him would ultimately dissolve given enough time in a hard rain, it still seemed to him, in that moment, to be more durable than most of the buildings he had passed that morning.

In his apartment, facing an unadorned and wiped-clean table, Timon began the task of dissection. The seams steadied and then stretched taut by left thumb and pointer. From the right hand came the blade to prompt the package's dismantling. He noted Sarja's return address, an old neighborhood in Quebec City. It was not the first package Sarja had sent, though the two had never met—all Timon knew of this particular client was his age, and even that was vague, composed of conjectures formed after an unexpectedly late night of drinks on the East Coast with his father and uncle, two years before.

The first layer cleared, Timon sloughed the box away from its core—something encased in a skeletal three-dimensional frame and huddled between glistening plastic sacs of air. His father had always been fond of elaborate packaging, as though some other self, some other world's architect version of Timon's father had bled through, scattering some talents on his counterpart. Here, this scaffold surrounded something older, perhaps a sculpture or a sort of pottery. A tablet, Timon saw, but not something ancient. Rather, a fragment, bone-white and abstractly patterned, no language recognizable in the carvings. Beside it, a compact disc in a carrier and jottings in Timon's father's scrawl. *Northern Fragment Recordings* in fragmentary handwriting.

Beside the two objects stood the usual complement of documents and images, reference points and starting points. It came to him, what this was, coming through his mental fog suddenly, a capsule memory a few weeks old. Yannick Sarja's company had located a set of elderly audio recordings in a vault on the outskirts of Quebec City, sitting beside a few objects, the shard among them, in a safe deposit box. Sarja believed this to be evidence of an inventor, Henry Pärn, and been known to have lived in the area a century earlier, who had experimented in the early days of recorded audio, and dabbled in unorthodox disciplines.

"His interest in this is mainly for academic reasons," Timon's father had said. "Should it be legitimate, it's something to be bequeathed. A gift to an institution, his name in the papers—a patron, and a laudable one at that." Here, the firm stood as a bulwark—their instincts determining whether the recording merited passage for formal verification or was revealed as a strange curiosity and nothing more. This was Timon's particular talent, a sensitivity to small details and knowledge grafted onto him to match his own inborn inclinations. And so, in this case, a simple assignment: listen to this recording and determine whether the speaker's diction was consistent with the assumption: an Estonian taught French by the Québécois.

The fragment beside the recording was a supplement, packaged along with it because it had been found beside it, on the off chance that its own contours and components might prove revelatory. There was precedent for this: Timon's father matching a wooden frame to its maker, and thus naming a likely forger; his uncle tying white sands in a shirt pocket to the space of that same name in New Mexico; Timon himself registering a photograph in the background of a photograph as the early work of a transgressive artist, and from there filling in state, city, neighborhood, block, direction of the light, the year, the season, the week, the time of day.

And after that had been done, they signed off on their work, gathered the materials strewn before them, swaddled them and bound them and prepared to return

them to their origins. Forms and documents were readied
and stamped, and sometimes customs declarations were
made. Timon had heard from his father that an intern now
graced the halls of the New York office, walking discreetly.
Timon wondered just how far someone from outside the
family might progress in this particular framework.

"We watch the liturgy together sometimes," his father
had said, and Timon had nodded despite the continent
between them.

And now Timon turned his attention to the recording.
He took the disc from its case and walked it to his alcove
and pulled audio into his computer. After a while playback
came, and Timon sat in a high-backed chair and listened.
First there was static, a tower made from it, or perhaps
a wave, rolling toward him out of speakers and instantly
filling the room. It was as though the walls had been made
irrelevant; as though the sheets of overburdened sound had
taken it upon themselves to redefine the boundaries of his
living space. Timon's proximity to the sound concerned
him: it seemed to him to be too much, too immediate;
he stood and walked to the center of the room, a place
where the sound might gather around him and where his
observations might be made with clarity.

Timon sought something in the sound—some strand
of recognition, of notes or words or sounds from which he
could render meaning. He wondered whether he wasn't
listening deftly enough, if the transfer of the recordings
was perhaps flawed in some substantial way, when the
words began, a whisper through a smoke-filled room. The

words settled on Timon, and as they first came to rest on him their language seemed impenetrable. They seemed like collections of glottal sounds, of syllabic patterns devoid of meaning.

He stood, centered in the room, waiting. The clip ran for three minutes and then repeated. By the third repetition, Timon could confirm the language as French, could comprehend a few key phrases. He stood in the center of the room and let the words hit and hit and hit, their rhythm unceasing. After ten listens he felt that he could comprehend the entire recording—or at least what could be understood, certain of its words having been lost to the vagaries of the process or to a general decay having borne down on the recording as it waited in isolation.

As he stood in it, Timon began to file details, to isolate and prepare and dissect sounds that emptied suffering and rebuilt walls. A thought of his father's note: "An Estonian taught this language by a Québécois scholar." His proof to find or dismantle, then. Soft cadences stumbling. Timon was proceeding back out of meaning and analysis; beyond words, digesting words back into components, compositing words and consonants and autopsying the residue. For seven sessions he heard only patterns, a return to rises and falls and pauses. Timon inhaled and sank into its substance, into its surface, and he settled in, his thoughts returning to old linguistic tracts, field recordings, and curated ethnography.

It ran again, this phrase, on him now like oxygen or ozone. A foregone science, no subject he'd studied save in some preternatural womb that drifted over most of his life. Timon's father had often spoken of instinct, of how he had been raised under theories of instinct, of a reaching out and a reconnection to something seeded years before. And here, Timon was beginning to see it, to visualize transit, this imagined speaker's journey from the Baltic to ice-riven Canadian walls, and of the age at which the Estonian might have begun his studies of this new language. An early year, Timon decided. The theoretical Estonian had undertaken his studies from a young age. And so—an instinctual grasp of tenses and verbs and the appropriate placement of adjusted adjectives? And so the Estonian grew in his mind, in it a middle-aged man trekking through Europe, socially adept across a score of nations.

In the twenty-sixth repetition of the speaker's words, Timon began to detect stumbles in the grammar. Stumbles that he himself, speaking French—or, for that matter, Estonian—might have made. Here a half-cough, there a pause as an appropriate word, a just word, was sought. And by the twenty-seventh, the flaws became even fuller, this tapestry more crude. Halts and drags and a faint probing search, some other grammar bleeding in the hesitant patterns.

The static had nearly abated, had come to be indistinguishable from the room's architecture. There was the room and the room's echo, its slipcover, this fantasy of sudden deliverance. And on some level, Timon knew that when the recording was inevitably silenced, when his hand rose to cease the speaker's repetition, the static would snap back into silence, and he would stumble in the manner of a man whose crutch was displaced by a swift diagonal kick.

But for now the state remained, for now the room was wreathed in it, the voice the garland. A few more passes, a few more cycles, before Timon could be sure, could telephone his father in the east and say with certainty that this recording was not the work of Henry Parn, that Yannick Sarja's curiosity was merely a curiosity and no mean revelation. And then would come forms his signature, the guarantee of his instinct—which Timon still took as a strange concept, but it did earn him his keep—and the deft repackaging of the recording and its accompanying detritus.

This was all to come. For now, Timon stood in the path of words that were now simply sounds, no decision made. For in the words' fall, they slipped from grounding, evading all categorization, and could no longer prompt associations or trigger affiliations. He stood in the alien sounds and the familiar state and felt relief, felt everything other than relief drain from him and leave him empty save a quiet succor.

4

TIMON'S THURSDAY NIGHT ROUTINE: a careful drone, a subdued sort of activity that he conducted in solitude and silence. It was a bastardized contortionism, resembling to a theoretical onlooker nothing quite so much as someone's flawed idea of pilates: a series of movements both less intensive and more theatrical than the actual discipline. In fact, Timon's contortion was part of a routine, and had been fairly consistent for the past eighteen months. It had descended from his memories of an observed yoga, a lesson witnessed in a studio down the coast and a testimonial received later on; the sudden and all-consuming thought in Timon's mind that this was something he needed to do, a practice he needed to adopt. One night a few months later, he returned home whiskey-drunk and inspired and saw fit to diagram the routine. It was this combination of movements, executed at a meticulous pace, that he had undertaken at regular intervals in the days and weeks and months since then.

On some level, Timon understood that this system was flawed, or perhaps worse than flawed, but he remained at it, satisfied by the regular sense of nothingness it allowed him. It was an area in which he was not an expert. It was something that he could experimentally raise, a phantom discipline, something he could create in and out of solitude.

And so when the sound of the call trilled through his apartment at a point where he was halfway through his motions, the sense of being wrenched away from a point of beatific focus left him feeling halfway born, feeling a surreal anger that inhabited his tone, his manner, his choice of words. And so when he heard his father's voice saying, "We need to talk about this business in Charleston," Timon's initial response was to spit out something about his hatred of the city's palmetto bugs and humidity, before doubling back, coughing. "A rough night yesterday," he said by way of explanation, not quite an apology. Not for the first time, Timon wondered just what his family thought of his drinking, implied and otherwise.

"The Clarlignes have always been good to us," Timon's father said. "It's a historical thing. You know that. If we're talking about you or someone else visiting Charleston and dealing with some prehistoric-sized bugs, well, so be it."

Timon nodded, then stilled the phone. At some point, he had been able to converse with his family about matters familial and matters technical and keep the two separate: he could wish happy birthdays without the topic segueing into talk of contracts, or inquire about the state of distant cousins and not fear that he would be asked to board a plane in thirty-six hours for a distant city. All of that had changed at some point, a shift so subtle he found it impossible to denote, but he feared that some line had been crossed: that he was at once more the trusted associate and more the petulant child. He wondered for how long the two could coexist.

"What's the assignment proper?" asked Timon, and then cleared his throat. It seemed to him then that his words seemed terse and overly formal, birthing a tension requiring immediate dilution. Thus, coughs. Easier, Timon thought, than jokes.

"It's an antiques job," replied his father. "Matching some items, some heirlooms, in old photos with what the family thinks those items are today."

"And I'd need to go down there, you think?"

There was a pause on the other end of the line. "Maybe not. I'll see what I can do about getting anything transportable over to you out there. Photographs and… scans of letters, that sort of thing. Watch for it."

"Okay," said Timon.

"In about a week or so, I'll arrange a call between you and your contact for the Clarlignes. We're not sure yet if it's going to be Jonathan or the family's attorney. It's been informal so far, the talks we've had on it, but I'm sure we'll need to sign something or other before we can get the archives over to you."

Timon found himself nodding again, found himself
wishing that there was something he could say to
acknowledge what his father was saying in a neutral
manner, neither brusque nor overly casual.

"It'll be the usual Clarligne fee," said Timon's father.
"On completion, they'll hand off the check, either literally
or metaphorically. Send us a report, and confirmation of
your tithe."

And here Timon sighed, dredging up the same
frustrations he had hoped to bury at the start of the call.
"Really?" he said. "You know my feelings on the tithe."

"And you know ours," his father said. "The tithe isn't
up for negotiation."

After a pause, Timon said, "All right." His father said
the same and hung up. Standing alone in his apartment,
Timon remembered questions he had wanted to pose to his
father, remembered things he had hoped to ask about the
family entirely removed from the business, information
he had hoped to learn about a cousin's wedding, the sale of
a house, a few fresh addresses. He felt nerves and hunger
and a sudden and lasting restlessness.

Plates before them, Marianne's friends Esteban and Iris
talked about the storefront museum they planned to open.
It was a late dinner in Belltown, with Esteban taking the
evening's role of chef.

"I've been wondering what curry spices could do with
bacon," he said from the kitchen; that helped Marianne
to place the odors she detected hovering from there, an
almost sacrilegious succulence. She knew the both of

them from a grim cafe several miles away, one that they had all frequented during a time when they lived in other apartments. They had gotten to know one another over time through recognition of like-minded tastes. Books and T-shirts were identified and decoded and something vaporous had been determined to build upon that. Marianne had witnessed Iris and Esteban's slow shift from friendship to something else, and now to this, a comfortable cohabitation and an elusive intimacy. Esteban spoke about a vacant space he'd been eyeing for months now, spoke of proximity and foot traffic and how it called out for something unique. Iris picked up the thread and gestured, slipped in a few scenarios, balancing between her pride in her work and her frustrations with the time it required.

"I live a small-scale life," Iris said at one point as they sat, wine glasses and lips mottled red, the food at center-table devoured. "Still, I like thinking in terms of beams, of acres, of support structures and arches that span hundreds of feet. Sometimes that gets to me. I realize how much that dwarfs me, and it throws me off."

Marianne raised her glass to her lips and paused, thinking that she should say something in return. Nothing came to mind, and she drank after the stutter in her hand ceased. Her work seemed less adventurous, less meaningful, and she wondered what she could offer. She wondered if there was anything she could offer, and even whether there was anything that she *should* offer.

She thought about the open spaces at her own job, the occasional dawn-chasing night there, the quiet collegiality.

"It's funny," said Esteban. "Because I don't ever see that. I don't know if I'd know about that if you didn't tell me about it." And then he laughed, as though he realized the impracticality of what he was saying, and the flaws that it might open. "I guess what I'm saying is: you transition well."

"Yeah," Iris said, "but it helps, too. It helps because I can save those smaller spaces, I can keep them private. I can put things in them during the day and bring them to mind without reviving the day's stresses on me when I get back here. It's all right," she said. "It's all right."

Marianne looked on. The talk of distances sparked thoughts of atlases and demarcations of scale. She cleared her throat. "I used to collect maps," she said. "Something from everywhere I'd been. I used to think about breaking them down and, I guess, making art from them. Sometimes that seems utterly alien to me now, and sometimes it seems like the most natural thing I could do."

"Did you ever do anything like that?" Iris asked.

Marianne shook her head. "Well, maybe. There's a box somewhere, maybe in a storage space, that has a couple of older ones. I was just out of college then; I had no fixed location. I practiced a bit, I guess—studies for something that never got finished."

Iris said something to Marianne about how she'd love to see this work sometime, and Esteban agreed. Marianne thought about her half-formed case studies locked away somewhere to the north, thought about their assembly and how she thought to lose herself in it, of reassembly and collage carried out with no formal guidelines. It had brought a fleeting bliss, but that bliss was supplanted in time with vertiginous unease. She filed them away and let them idle; occasionally, her thoughts of them seemed to be the work of another.

The dinner plates were cleared and the red wine had given way to a port, recently acquired by Iris at a shop discovered while taking an alternate way home. The three of them were sitting on couches, and Marianne knew that if she stood at that moment she would sway. In some corner of her mind she felt shame and vowed to carry through, hoped that her car could be left overnight. Iris was speaking about colleagues of hers, peers whom she had met through the local chapter of the American Institute of Architects. "Sometimes—they do fantastic work, some of them. There's a space out here for that, for the experimental, for the things that seem impractical. This guy, Richard something, has been playing with modular housing, has commissions, has been talking about quitting, about doing that full-time."

Esteban's face puzzled. "But that's not—"

"No. Not at all. Maybe it's…I don't know." Iris's manner calcified, her demeanor summoning an academic gravity. "I guess it's the grass always being greener. It's something like that."

"What about," Marianne began, and then stopped. The idea had entered her head when she heard the word *modular*, and the words had lined themselves up—too formally, she realized as she began to speak them. She was among friends here, not a detective on an investigation. "This is going to sound strange," she said, addressing Iris, "but there's...do you know a coffee stand an hour north of here, just off the interstate, murals all over it?"

"It sounds familiar," said Esteban. His face still bore a quizzical appearance, and he had now squinted one eye closed. Iris, Marianne noted, was nodding.

"You don't happen to know who designed it, do you?" Marianne asked. Iris shook her head.

"I wish I did, though—if it's the one I'm thinking of, it's got a smart look to it." She paused. "Why do you ask?"

Marianne inhaled. "Couple of weeks ago, I thought I was going to punch this drunk asshole at a show I was at. He was flailing, doing everything I hate when I'm watching bands. Reeked of whiskey and vodka; there were...stains on his shirtsleeves."

"I think I remember you telling us about that," said Esteban, his face now relaxed. "Your confrontation."

"Well, I keep seeing evidence of him. His face on a mural on the coffee stand, for one. So I've been trying to find out more. Who he is, what he haunts. Why this berserk drunkard is important, basically." By the end of it, she noticed that both Iris and Esteban were looking at her, their expressions sobered. She herself felt more steady, felt clarity returning.

"This might sound strange," said Iris. "But why bother?"

"I don't know, really," said Marianne. "Maybe to take him down a peg. Maybe to unsettle him like he unsettled me. It's a behavior…you know how I feel about that." She breathed deeply, sounding it out. "My work's not as exciting as either of yours. Maybe I just need something that's a kind of mystery."

5

AFTER THREE DAYS OF waiting for documents, of expectations of newly-arrived packages clad in shrink-wrap and swathed in padding, conveyed in corrugated cardboard and transported via air freight, Timon received word that Jonathan Clarligne would instead be bringing the materials to him directly. The younger Clarligne would be in Seattle the following day, Timon was told, for reasons unrelated to this assignment. Timon's father had called with the news. "Buy him a meal," he said. "Somewhere generous. Impress him. And make sure you get a receipt." Timon acquiesced to this plan of events.

The night before Jonathan's arrival, the nature of their meeting still unclear, tentative plans circulated for a brief conversation at a sophisticated establishment, Timon ventured to a distant venue to watch a trio of bands clatter and roar their way through three-minute pop songs, sneers in tow; the chords played staccato, the vocals barked, the lyrics composed of accusations and denunciations. The beer present at the venue wasn't enough to get Timon drunk, and the beer wasn't enough to provoke movement. He stood toward the back of the space and nodded his head and wondered about running, either into the fray before the stage or for the door. The night and a handful of confused pedestrians would be there to greet him if he walked out front or stumbled out front.

He had met Jonathan Clarligne once before. Jonathan had been twenty, which still earned him the tag of prodigy. It had been in Los Angeles, and by chance: Timon had followed a friend of his there, had gone there to profess something like love, had been carefully deflated and had stumbled out of a bar at five in the afternoon not wanting any sort of company, no matter how politely an expression of honesty had been delivered. And halfway down the block, Jonathan Clarligne had been there, a face he knew from photographs and a name he knew from familial conversations. In Los Angeles for his sideline in business, Timon later learned, the genius-boy consultant. Jonathan had been at the center of a beautiful crowd and Timon had been devastated, and their conversation had been brief and formal and, if not traumatic for either man, than certainly something neither of them saw fit to repeat.

Timon occasionally heard rumors and legends of Jonathan Clarligne. Never via his parents, but through siblings, through colleagues he had met through the family business. Gossip clustered around Jonathan Clarligne like scab to a wound: talk of a child, talk of a brief marriage, of a dawn-lit Vegas wedding. Jonathan Clarligne had made an album in secret. Jonathan Clarligne had made an album in secret that was amazing; bootleg recordings circulating on file-sharing sites under half a dozen aliases. Jonathan Clarligne had left his family's firm in disgrace. Jonathan Clarligne had folded his consulting business in disgrace. Jonathan Clarligne had returned to the family's firm in prodigal fashion. Jonathan Clarligne had purchased a Manhattan apartment for an exorbitant sum. Timon heard all of them, declined to make assumptions about which were true and which were not. All he could say with certainty was that Jonathan Clarligne was his junior by several years and yet possessed the gravity of someone a generation older. This fact, unassailable, set Timon on edge.

Onstage, the band had taken up a song that invited the crowd to shake. Timon drained his beer and moved forward and decided to reciprocate. As he moved, his head bobbing and body twisting and legs, yes, shaking, he scanned the crowd and saw no one familiar. He rarely saw those he knew at shows such as this, but he never quite lost that hope, that flash that comes when one sees a familiar face transposed to a new environment and receives a gloried onrush of potential, a kind of renewal of faith. He kept moving for as long as he could before his energy flagged, his eyes still on those around him, hoping for some sense of recognition.

Marianne worked at a job that had not existed a decade
earlier. On sporadic visits to her family she often found
herself describing it in surreal terms, the disbelief
surrounding her fueling her own disbelief, a thought
burrowing away into her that this was somehow transient,
that this line of work was ephemeral, might vanish at any
point, that she might yet find herself in a telemarketing
cubicle or offering upgrades of fast food to disinterested
customers; these were the kinds of jobs friends of hers had
baited her with during her collegiate years, and those old
anxieties had never entirely left her. Marianne structured
websites, essentially: developed plans and charts and
outlines for how information might be navigated. She
had been in this job for three years and found a reliable
comfort in it.

In her office, she cued up a cover of "Wall of Death"
and listened to it again and again. It cleared her head, its
repetition summoning a sort of meditation, and soon she
was ready for the day's work: two meetings within the office
and one with a prospective client. A third meeting would
follow to discuss the result of that, and how the company's
interests might be advanced. There was, Marianne
supposed, an aptitude one should have for scenarios such
as this. She assumed on some level that she possessed
it, though never felt cognizant of it as such. There was a
comfort she took in travel, an ease in the moments when
she felt her life transitioning from one city to the next, and
a shelter triggered by the presence of maps. None of those
feelings arose here; the closest she came was the charting,

the creation of paths, the documentation of navigation. It never matched up; she felt at times like a documentarian shooting pop videos or a long-haul driver in an off-road vehicle. And yet there was an ease to it, and a comfort in that.

Sometime past eleven, her boss Archer knocked on her door. Archer had an old-money look: he always dressed impeccably, tailored suits that stood in sharp contrast to the casual appearance of the rest of the office, a mode Marianne recognized from celebrity photo shoots and *New York Times* Men's Fashion supplements. He ushered himself in and, closing the door, began by saying, "I wouldn't be putting this on you if we didn't believe you couldn't do it."

Marianne counted the negatives and hoped she had correctly interpreted that which Archer was trying to say, then considered that Archer himself was stumbling. She thought of his expression and trusted in that. "We have a meeting today with a prospect. Not a firm that's universally known, but one that has prestige; more to the point, we're also talking about a not-insignificant amount of money to add to our proverbial coffers. Apparently, the fellow we're meeting with is also something of a patron, so there's been talk of that trickling down into something as well."

Marianne nodded. "So how do I figure into this?" she asked. "I don't normally get involved until the dotted line has been signed."

"I know," said Archer. "I know. But the usual crew that handles these is down a couple: Whitsun's on his honeymoon and Renata's on maternity leave. And I'd say you're good at eyeing people, good at sussing people out. And you know what we're about, and you can hold a decent conversation."

Marianne did not dispute any of this. "So do we have information on them? I think I should research some of this."

"I'll send it over," said Archer. "The meeting will be offsite—the theoretical client gets into town in a few hours, so he's asked that we meet him at his hotel's restaurant. Five-thirty's the start time; I'll be by at six." Marianne looked at him quizzically. "Board meeting," he said, his cheeks reddening. Archer was on at least five, by Marianne's count: two charities, two arts organizations, and something that existed in a realm of the nebulously well-off, an entity that clung to the affluent and seemed to exist in conditions perceptible only to them.

She traveled home at lunch to find clothing more suited to the coming meeting. She worked until four-thirty, reading about the firm whose emissary she was slated to meet, searching for additional information on them, and readying the materials she hoped to have on hand for their meeting. She had been invited to a handful of these over the years, though never as the primary representative, and their formality and content differed radically from client to client.

At five-fifteen, a cab pulled up outside their office to convey her to a downtown hotel. She stepped inside and walked toward the agreed-upon meeting place. The restaurant and bar were nearly empty, and so her contact was easy to locate. Seated in a booth was a fresh-faced young man with a gleam in his eyes, his clothing the Platonic ideal to which Archer's aspired. A manila folder and a laptop sat on the table before him; Marianne placed his age at twenty-four, and a young-looking twenty-four at that. Beside the young man sat a woman dressed casually, tall and thin, with short red hair tied severely atop her head, some strands beginning to make their escape. Marianne introduced herself and sat. Her contact indicated his companion.

"This is Dana," said Jonathan Clarligne. "She's a muralist."

6

TIMON WOKE AT FIVE-THIRTY on the morning of his meeting with Jonathan Clarligne. They were to receive cocktails at a bar near Seattle Center that evening. Timon knew of the place, and had set foot inside once or twice a year or two ago, during the time when his last relationship of any immediacy had been in its dying spasms. The couple had stepped into the bar and seated themselves and attempted diplomacy, as though Old Fashioneds and specialty bitters might serve as tonic for the fracture that bore down on them.

Timon took time to recollect all of this the night before, an hour or so before allowing sleep to take him. Had he recalled the bar's name before then, he might have suggested a different meeting place to Jonathan Clarligne, but by now it was too late; by now he had no choice but to attire himself in the garb of a more sophisticated man, to

steady his hands and allow himself the ability to assume
something resembling luxury.

Five-thirty, though. Eyes opened to a dark sky, and
that moment of panic, of irrational fear of an eighteen-
hour sleep. And the attempts to return to that state,
alarms arrayed 'round his bed to wake him at a more
sensible hour, one not shared with captains of industry
and salarymen on East Coast time. He lay there, his eyes
unwilling to close, still staring at the cold blank sky. There
was a cursory review before the meeting, Timon pondered,
but that could be accomplished anywhere papers could be
set before him and a few notes jotted on a pad. The true
work would be invoked at the meeting and begin after
the meeting, once Jonathan Clarligne had offered up his
documents and his images and bade him commence. And
so Timon decided to stand and shower and then make the
drive down the interstate to Olympia for breakfast.

The morning birthed foggy: Timon at a quarter past
six, southbound on Interstate 5. He went for narcoleptic
music in the car, chords like driftwood colliding with the
shore. Six forty-five and he was free from Seattle's well. He
felt the road open itself to greet him, the fog still present
with coal-gray clouds above. Old mixtapes and demos
from bands that had practiced around the block from his
former office rested in the center compartment, and after a
while he thumbed through them, his hands coming to rest
on a familiar one, atmospheres with violin cutting through
them, seemingly endless looping melodies. It fit the
weather, he thought. Good music for jarring connections

free, to let them drift into air. He drank the last of the coffee cupped beside the gearshift and continued south.

By seven-thirty, he had parked and was walking anonymous in Olympia. Timon surveyed his curved reflection in car windows: the neutral jacket, the neutral hair. He thought, that right there is a man who looks restrained. He moved on, the windows in which he watched himself gradually moving from automotive curvature to storefront translucent sheets, slipping down into pavement only to be met by metal restraints. Around him there was movement on the streets: students awake before early classes, bodies a few years older moving down sidewalks, running errands or breaking for coffee before the day's work began. Neither operated in a mode that matched Timon's own: he felt formally nondescript, professionally median. The corners became more familiar, the sounds from passing cars easing him into a tempo he understood. Around another corner was a diner at which he could pass the time, could ready the words and the offers necessary when dealing with Jonathan Clarligne.

As he walked through the diner's door, recognition blindsided Timon like a hunter's club: the same relationship that had clued him in to the cocktail bar at which he would find himself later that night had also been his first reason for coming here. Second broadcasts of disquieting thoughts struck him again; notably, that half of his knowledge of the state had come from her. That even now as he went about his business, his business and his family's business, he was in some way tracking in grooves that had long since worn down. It seemed to him, as he was ushered to his seat and a mug of coffee set before him, that it was strange that their paths had rarely overlapped since the break. Still the occasional glances at crowded rooms, still the sporadic events for which their tastes had overlap. Their corridors dwelt mainly in parallel; for Timon, that was almost adequate.

She had hated the tithe as well, Timon remembered as he paged through the menu, as he zeroed in on the morning's meal. She had hated his ties to the family firm, had urged him to quit it, had raised countermeasures and offered up scenarios and solutions in order to extricate him from that life. Their time together seemed to him now to have been an arrangement of paradoxes: the work that had allowed him entry to Seattle was the same work that had led to the unraveling of the sole occasion he had for intimacy in that city. His own rushes and need for strange and infuriated contact were not the source of horror to her that it was for others, but were rather the wellspring of a fascination and an attraction and, perhaps, of inspiration. He ate and regarded his papers. At one point his gaze lifted and he looked toward the windows. Outside, the cloud cover had not departed, and now their low diffuse sprawl seemed to promise rain. In the glass, Timon found his reflection's eyes and met them. He looked at himself: a man hunched over a plate, nondescript and of little obvious purpose. And after a while, he returned to the information before him, letting it drift into his eyes and waiting for connections to form.

Marianne arrived home after her meeting with Clarligne
to find her data connection temporarily fractured, her
ability to delve for information from home hobbled. With
that truncation came a sort of frustration: she needed to
see Dana's art. To have asked about it when discussing
business with Clarligne, she knew, would have been
improper. Dana had sat and watched the meeting, as
though she had acted as a particularly creative bodyguard:
the sort who would effortlessly fell a threat to one's person,
then sculpt their own rendition of the intended attack.

Dana and Clarligne had possessed the sort of
ambiguous intimacy that caused Marianne endless
frustration. It was never readily apparent to her, those who
embodied this condition: half the time she would learn of
their status as lovers and feel confident in her assumptions,
a lasting teenage pride in that quality of recognition. But
there were also the times when she had been wrong: when
she had casually said to mutual friends, "They're together,
right?" and received a bewildered look, as though she had
raised suggestions of incest or something less conceivable,
of a relationship beyond the mind's ability to process.

And so she woke early that morning to a streaked city.
She clad herself in a jacket and checked that her windows
were closed and began the trek toward work. The trees
she passed were bent low like supplicants and mourners.
She was the third to arrive at the office that day, behind
the partner who thought it appropriate to live on Eastern
Standard Time, and the new guy, all sharp sideburns and
Western shirts, early enough in his tenure that he was

still eager to please. Marianne keyed in Dana's name and began her search.

Dana's full name was shared with the owner of a pet supply store in Nebraska, a British swimmer, a professor at a small Baptist college. Marianne followed all of them, as each retained just enough plausibility to warrant the time. After ten minutes, her suspicions were confirmed: the store owner was seemingly in her sixties; the swimmer, sixteen; and the professor had in fact given a lecture the previous night on a campus two thousand miles away.

Another twenty minutes passed before Marianne found anything that seemed likely. Some photographs on a hand-coded page collecting pictures of murals were credited to Dana Guterson. While Marianne had never been a precise scholar of artistic movements or periods, these were clearly the work of the same artist whose mural she had encountered on the road to Anacortes. There was nothing else featuring the drunkard, however; his face or contortions marred no other pictured work. As she cycled though Dana's work, Marianne found the drunkard to be increasingly irrelevant; instead, she studied the evolution of a style, the way in which lines were formed and connected, the layering of Krylon atop a subtly melting coat of oil. This is what beckoned her in; this is what prompted languorous stares long after she realized that work's demands hovered just to her side.

7

ON THE EVENING OF his meeting with Jonathan Clarligne, Timon wanted nothing more than simple inebriation. His day had been spent inside, primarily at his desk, trying to avoid the temptations of the rest of his apartment, trying to defer his own impulses telling him to run from this project, to run from the Clarligne account and the business and all that it encompassed. He threw on a jacket over a rakishly cut shirt that Dana had urged him to buy, had told him he wore well. He eyed himself in the mirror and saw nothing more or less of a particular mode than the clothes he had worn earlier in the day. He looked in the mirror and saw a man in need of a pocket watch. The thought unsettled him.

He set out from his apartment on foot. The air outside seemed suited to a long walk, even an uphill one. He had not lived in this city long enough for every walk over a certain distance to not strike him as inherently angled upward. He felt a steady and consistent forty-five degrees off the sidewalks and roads he had come of age walking. He felt unsettled here, still. As he walked, as his body became weighed upon by forces at odd angles, he thought, People who grew up here don't feel it this way. This disorientation is the toll they pull from us, the migrants, those who came here from elsewhere. I would not know this push-pull urging collapse had I remained in the east.

Still. Then, in motion. The ascent, a slight perspiration on his forehead the only indication of the length of his trek. The conveyance westward after a series of conversations with his father. Two bottles of red wine mostly gone and a night watching spring emerge on the Eastern Seaboard and a cough and the question: "What's the furthest I can go from here and still work for the business?" And the answer, without hesitation: "Seattle." Timon had rehearsed it for weeks, had researched cities and retrieved data, amassed a folly of glyphs and monuments and potential outcomes. And yet his words had come through him like a spontaneous conversion, with his father's response measured, a close cousin to a prepared statement. He had given the matter some thought on the drive out, and then buried it below other concerns. And in recent weeks, it had come back to him, an unruly haunting that flooded his thoughts and bore witness to the tithe.

His ascent was nearly over. He was passing an art school now, and in a block he would be past it. He knew its name from idle conversations at parties and, briefly, from the time he had entertained hiring someone. A

rental of office space, someone to sit at an adjoining desk;
a companion and a compatriot—a notion with which he
had been infatuated since his arrival in the city. Instead,
the decision to reinforce the home office, to go it alone.
The desk and the computer and the halfhearted view. Call
it pragmatism: it brought with it its own frustrations, but
Timon had learned long ago how to temper those.

The restaurant named by Jonathan Clarligne as their
meeting grounds looked unfinished. The name CAMP
REVIVAL was halfway etched above the door. As Timon
walked inside, his attention was pinched by the sight of
towering grain-filled prints hanging at regular intervals
on the walls, four feet high and almost square in shape.
In each of them, he could see the shapes of tents. In some
they were in the foreground, a series spread across a grass
field. In others they were a distant presence, a sea; in
others that sea stood divided beside an ocean. The faces
in the photographs were full of elation and gratitude; in
some, Timon could see ecstasy.

In the restaurant, someone was approaching. Timon
knew it was Clarligne before he registered Clarligne but
it was the photographs which continued to occupy his
attention, setting him to catalog and lend translation.
Ocean Grove, he thought. *Ocean Grove in 1938* came to
him first; then he began to register details that solidified
that. The contours of a car and the wear on the side of
a building he had passed in his youth, in the days when
his father's tithe brought with it a pilgrimage. The clarity
of the photographs allowed for certain luxuries: a handful

of discernible banners, a poster hanging on a lamppost. He pocketed this information and forced it to become compressed, a form he could slide into his hand like a magician's scarf. Timon extended his hand to Jonathan Clarligne. "Always a pleasure," said Timon. After a few moments, he nodded.

"There's a table in the back," said Jonathan Clarligne. As they walked, Timon wished for blinders. His eyes wanted the images on the walls. Look at them for long enough, he thought, and he would recognize the film from the grain, could venture a guess as to the conditions under which they were taken—the sunniness of the day, the brightness of sun on sand. He watched Jonathan Clarligne walk and stared at the back of his neck, watched the fibers of his suit and the edge of the shirt that it covered. Timon had made it a point to learn as little as he could about clothing: his own instruction was regimented so as to reliably clad him in an understated mode. If it had been conceived or sewn in the last half-century, it represented a precious void to him, and the thought of it brought him to a state approaching intoxication.

Jonathan Clarligne brought him to a table, a minimal square pushed up from the floorboards by a pole. At Clarligne's setting was a spherical glass of red wine, its consumption marked by red threads traced on the inner surface. The color brought Timon to grief. From the speakers came a Steve Reich composition, reprocessed and redistributed, volume monitored to prevent disorientation. Timon eased his chair back and twisted into it, and Jonathan Clarligne did the same. From a satchel by the floor, he withdrew a taut envelope and passed it across the table. "Charleston," he said. "We found them in a building we owned, during renovations that were being made to it." He swallowed nothing in particular, the motion bobbing his neck forward and the sigh that followed returning his poise. "Less renovation, I suppose, than a kind of demolition."

Timon took up the envelope and opened it, sliding his finger under the seal, the contact leaving a small bloody nick beside his fingerprint's whorl. Inside were a stack of photographs, some with black marker notes on the back, and papers, a lengthy numbered list paperclipped together. His unmarred fingers paged through them and, preparing for the review, he licked his cut and rubbed it idly on his napkin. "Do you mind?" he said to Jonathan Clarligne and, when the other man ushered his hands forward, began to spread the contents of the envelope on the table before him.

"I remember your father telling me you were fond of a well-aged bourbon," Timon heard from across the table. Already he was vanishing into the photographs, transparent hands spreading them in triptychs on the table. Peripheral vision brought signs of a motion to him: Jonathan Clarligne in the last stages of a nod. He stared at the images, studied the composition of each in turn. Studied loose outlines of figures, fragments in the frame, and the textures, and the grain. There would be time enough for detail, for the savoring and supposition.

A sudden flatness struck Timon, gloss where none should be. "These are copies," he said. "Not just prints." He raised his head from its study, coughed, and spoke. "They have the look of the third generation to them."

"The originals—they might not be the originals, but our originals—are in Charleston. We haven't trusted the airlines with anything since the problem with the recorder last April." Timon returned a shrug that conceded the point. Contemplation resumed, a standard left-to-right evaluation. The first of the three in the first row of two was, perhaps, the oldest. In it, a child stood. Instincts said Prohibition: clothing style and masonry and the look of the focus, the look of the eyes. The child was male, ten or eleven; he held a gun, pointed it toward something in the leftward distance. The child's face was neutral.

The second photograph was of a wedding. As was the third, Timon gathered, and possibly the fifth. Late 1930s, lantern-lit, formal dress and many drinks already downed. Guests, he saw. None of them the couple at the event's heart. A smiling man, his hand on one strand of lanterns, the other beckoning. The next photograph featured the same man, his arm around a woman of similar height, her hair long, probably red, her eyes meeting the lens and enriching it.

Fourth image: possibly a monochrome print of color film. A church wall, a body laying in state. Corpse hands, suit-clad, united in prayer in the image's lower-left corner. Filling the upper-right corner, filling most of the photograph, was a stained-glass window, intricate in design. The window's image: a man in a cloak offering an open hand to a bird in a tree, the tree bearing fruit, light shining through glass-flesh and pear-shape.

The fifth image was a wedding of roughly the same period as the previous two. A tree-stump of a man stood on a balcony, a cigarette in one hand, his necktie loosened. With his free hand, he was pulling back his suit jacket; with the smoking hand, he was indicating something on his shirt. Timon drew closer, as though proximity might somehow cause the film to grow sharper, as though it might summon the photographer's ghost to declaim pertinent issuances. The shirt was torn, Timon concluded. The shirt fell on flesh unmarred, but the shirt was nonetheless cut. Twice, Timon decided.

The eyes Timon saw in the sixth photograph convinced him in moments that he was beholding the child from the first image. All other details fell away: he did not look to the background to date it or to styles of clothing or novels in hand or posters in shopwindows. This was the boy who had held a shotgun, now at least twenty years older, wearing robes and clerical collar, a determined look on his face, blonde hair forming a widow's peak. Timon looked up at Jonathan Clarligne. "Same one," he said. Then he arranged his fingers, one pointer above each of the two photographs in which the priest appeared. "This one," he said. "Became this one."

"That's good to hear," said Jonathan Clarligne. "But really, we're more concerned about the shotgun."

Timon looked ahead of him, locking Jonathan Clarligne in a quiet stare. He felt the part of a sprinter having arrived unexpectedly to a swim meet. He felt unexpected.

"This is the order in which we found them," said Jonathan Clarligne. One hand reached out and then drew back in a truncated croupier's wash. "And there's a dealer we know, traffics in elder firearms. And he says he knows something, has seen this one before. And its worth is abundant."

Timon felt formality enter him. "How do we compliment this arrangement?" he asked.

"Verification," said Jonathan Clarligne. "There's history in these photographs, and there's definitely history in that shotgun."

"Who's the child?" asked Timon. "You know who he is."

Jonathan Clarligne shrugged. "He's a bishop now. My mother's cousin. It's family business, I suppose, but it always is."

At home, Timon removed that which he was wearing and adopted a new look: monochromatic, flat, anonymous. He withdrew a bottle of vodka from his freezer and poured a shot and took it down. Its chill filled his sinuses with a feeling of hurtling toward some expanse, an underdressed downhill racer, his transit chaotic. Timon thumbed through local listings and zeroed in on something appropriate, something suitable for his mood, and headed there on foot. From outside the venue, he heard striking sounds from an organ and a guitar slowly escalating. He handed over eight dollars at the door and stepped inside and walked toward the bar. Six dollars transacted, and he had bourbon to nurse, complementing the sound that filled his ears. Timon turned his head toward the stage. There, the band was completing their set, their final song given the appropriate crescendos, the predicted buildup and sendoff, the anticipated payoff, the moment when everything is stripped raw, when players grew flayed and tempos crumbled. Timon always loved last songs.

And then the song was over and the soundman cued a Kentucky Pistol song for the entr'acte; one band began collecting their equipment as the next drew theirs close to the stage in preparation to unfold, to assemble, to prepare. Timon walked to the bar and ordered a fresh bourbon and drained it and smiled down the bar at a woman he didn't know, who promptly turned away. He ordered a fresh bourbon, and twenty-five minutes later he was in the midst of it, alcohol running down his chin and numbing skin like anesthetic's rub before a root canal.

He ran in circles, occasionally pushing against the bodies of others, his mind drawn again and again to a taller man, rail-thin, standing at the circle's fringes, long sleeves for this weather, hands in his pockets. Timon considered disruption and, after a minute hesitation, proceeded, digging into this man a fraction harder than he had to the others. The thin man looked over and glared and pushed back and Timon smiled an unjust smile and proceeded, hoping he might draw this man out before it was time to refresh himself at the bar. Another pass completed, Timon reached out to shove again, and from behind him Timon heard words take shape, disparaging words funneled at him though their specific cadences were indistinct. He shoved again and the man shoved back and the crowd around them sensed the beginning of a confrontation. The band continued to play. Timon grasped at the thin man and pulled him in and the thin man held one palm up as he came, reaching out toward Timon's throat, and so Timon paused and thought it best to unburden himself and moved to throw the thin man, to shift his weight and somehow release him. The thin man took his free hand and grasped Timon's wrist and looked at him with an expression of fury, unadorned fury, and now the band had stopped and Timon heard a concerned voice over the speakers—the vocalist, he assumed— saying, "Is everything okay in there? We don't want to see this at one of our shows," and Timon thought that perhaps a spiral might work the best. Around him the crowd was drawing back and someone was moving toward both of them, samaritan or bouncer, and Timon went carefree and estimated weights and was certain he could outmaneuver the thin man and began to rotate, leaning his body to the right and hoping to end this fight before it began, to allow for tumbling and collisions and then to leave, to retreat toward another bar or to the vodka in his freezer. And then there was a blur in his peripheral vision, his left eye saw something, and then his skull was bursting, his sense of the space he was in became swollen, the room abruptly turning bubble-shaped and then contracting. His hand released its grasp on the thin man's shirt and he fell backward and no one caught him and the music started up again. As he dropped, he saw two sets of arms holding the thin man back; he dropped and he hit the ground and things faded. His next memory was twenty minutes and three blocks away, stumbling into a brick wall, vomit already cast across shoes and ankles.

8

THE AFTER-WORK HOURS OF Marianne's Tuesdays generally found her meeting friends for dinner, generally at a bar with agreeable fare or at a coffee shop where smaller, yet more satisfying, portions could be found. Her partner on this particular Tuesday was Elias, and their dining space was one in Ballard, better known for its coffee than its food. As she walked through the door, she saw that Elias had already secured a table, had already procured beverages for them both. As she sat, she noticed that he was rubbing one hand with the other. Before raising her cup, she asked, "What happened?"

From Elias, a sigh. "I had to box a guy's ears the other night." To her stare, he added, "Unavoidable. He wanted a fight and I wanted to watch the band." He gestured, halfway to a raised eyebrow, and went to take a sip of his drink. "Look. They didn't throw me out, if that tells you anything."

"They threw him out, then?"

"I assume. I didn't see him around after that."

Marianne sighed, then reached for her coffee. She grazed the cardboard shell of the cup and drew her hand back. "What's on your mind?" she heard Elias say. She looked up at him.

"The usual at work," she replied. "The usual there. I'm helping Iris and Esteban with something this weekend. Staying home a lot. It's becoming a template."

"You feel like another road trip?" said Elias. "I've been meaning to get another tattoo, one I'm actually happy with. Lady who does them moved up north a few years ago, lives out in the woods somewhere." He rolled one shoulder back and idly glanced away. Marianne wondered what had pulled his attention away; Elias had never been one for stray glances.

Elias rolled both of his shoulders, then focused back on Marianne. "I was thinking of camping for a day or two, then cleaning myself up and heading in." One hand skipped over another like flint idly striking a rock. "Might be a time."

"It might," she said like a reflex. Half of what she was saying these days sounded to her like reflex responses, flowchart conversations she fell into readily. There was a guy halfway across her office whose desk she passed on the way to make coffee, and every few days she would hear him talking, essentially preaching, about the Turing test, about how he was going to be the one who built something to overwhelm it.

Elias hadn't said anything in response. He sat there, one hand now reposed atop the other, a grateful stillness on his face. She could hear the door opening and the sound of rain newly falling on the sidewalk outside, the sounds pedestrians made hastening to their destinations and yet looking to avoid a tumble. "What's the tattoo you're thinking of getting?"

He held up his wrist and pulled down the sleeve of his shirt, showing her blank skin. "Here," he said, his finger marking the spot. "In the smallest letters she can do. One word." There was a birthday-boy grin starting to take shape on him now. A brightening.

"What's the word?" Marianne asked.

"'Stakes,'" said Elias.

A day later, seated at work, Marianne decided to call Dana Guterson. Her notebook sat on the surface of her desk, open to sketches structuring the project she had undertaken for Jonathan Clarligne. From a few desks over, she heard her boss on the phone with someone. "Exactly," he was saying. "When I was in Prague, I ate at a restaurant called Reykjavik, and I knew my next trip had to be to Reykjavik. And when I went to Reykjavik, I flew to Helsinki and I ate at a restaurant called Santa Fé. Right, exactly. And that's where I met Bernadette. No, not in Helsinki. No, she was in Santa Fé for a conference and I was there...well, the sad thing is, I was there looking for a restaurant named for somewhere else."

Marianne pulled out her box, a patterned tin box that she had bought at a roadside market somewhere

that turned out to have fit the contours of a business card
perfectly. Her hands stopped at Dana Guterson's card and
she pulled it toward her, nestled it in her keyboard.

Marianne had dated a printmaker for much of her
time at college. Gainesville had been her home for four
years, and for a span of two and a half she had liaised with
a quiet man named Henry Benson, known to most of his
friends as Hermano. She had never entirely understood
that: Henry spoke four words of Spanish, if that, and had
no siblings whatsoever. He was a lifelong resident of the
city; they had met while watching a Blacktop Cadence
show, two sets of eyes resting on one another while throats
were torn and hearts exposed from the stage. There had
been a mutual decision made in those moments, a rapid
recognition of attraction that each soon understood, and
things had proceeded accordingly.

They had parted ways in her final year of college, at
first amicably, then not. He was still living in Florida,
making a living from teaching a few courses and
spending his off hours in isolation, layering colors atop
text, studying the effects of different sorts of ink on
different sorts of surfaces, losing himself in textures and
treatments. Through mutual friends, they had begun to
correspond; intimacy had, years later, birthed something
a half-step between acquaintance and friendship. She was,
she wagered, the only person aside from his students who
called him Henry.

The picture of Henry, and of Henry's pictures, came
to her unbidden as she stared at Dana Guterson's card. It

entered through a small hesitation: through an anxiety at impropriety, at the notion that contacting a client's companion might be taken the wrong way, might lead to a tremor, a weakening of certain aspects of her life, a collapse of rafters. A subtly triggered breakdown. And so she considered: might Dana Guterson and Henry Benson travel in similar circles? And still she eyed the card before her. She considered countries lost from maps, boundaries erased from edition to edition, capitals she had memorized in her youth for nations that no longer existed.

And she reached for the phone and dialed Dana Guterson's number and left a taut message, leaving her home number, before hanging up. She stood and filled a glass full of water and stood drinking it, surveying the cubicles and cubby-holes of the office around her.

Timon feared the port of Charleston. The family had had a house there once, his mother's academic life transporting her there, and as an inland-raised northerner, he found the avenues of the city theoretically fascinating yet, ultimately, distracting: an overlap of details that left his mind leaping from reference to reference, a massed set of associations that left him longing for night, for shattered streetlamps or a looming fog.

He had flown there from Seattle four times, and the quality of each visit had depended on which of his relatives had been waiting to greet him at the airport. His mother had been present once, and the visit had been a stable one, handshakes and the occasional embrace and clear meanings, a dearth of business and an abundance of quiet, four cars converging on a restaurant or pier; long drives up or down the interstate. At other times, his father had awaited him as he stepped into the baggage claim area, and those visits had been different, concentrations of meetings, temporary desks in clients' offices. The fitful sensation of being constantly monitored.

In the end, his father recommended that Timon visit Charleston as part of the Clarligne job. "You can do it without it," he said, "but you shouldn't." And so Timon eyed airfares and allowed his mind to wrap itself around the question of the imaged shotgun, and of what it might mean. It was one o'clock in the afternoon. Jonathan Clarligne, recently returned to the Carolinas, would certainly be available. It would be no intrusion for Timon to call, to announce his planned visit, to propose dates. But first he stood and walked into his kitchen and opened the refrigerator. A fading lightbulb shone on a glass bottle of water, three cans of beer, and a depleted carton of eggs. He took one of the beers, opened it, and walked back to his desk. Three times he drank from it before dialing Jonathan Clarligne. He would fly in two days, it was decided, Seattle to New York, New York to Charleston. A hotel room would be provided.

It was an early flight, preceded by a five-thirty cab ride through a fogged-in city. The highway brought no relief; from the back of the taxicab Timon watched headlights shafting through the shroud and nestled himself lower in his seat. "It's a fucking grim morning," said the driver. Timon grunted assent. "I remember mornings like this forty years ago. Crisscross the valley we'd go, my brother and me, a harvest stacked in the pickup." Timon took this neutrally and continued to listen; by the time they reached his terminal at Sea-Tac, the driver's narrative had reached the year of Timon's birth. Timon handed him a few folded bills and exchanged them for a blank receipt. He took his suitcase in hand and strapped bagged garments to one shoulder and began the walk to his gate.

As Timon understood it, he was the only member of his family unafraid to fly. He had traveled with his father on two work trips, and on each his father had asked Timon to wait for him outside the nondenominational chapel provided in the terminal. "Righting my soul," he told Timon. "In case of the worst. Bomber or bloodclot." The notions made Timon shudder, and he stood there, carry-on bag at his feet, book in his hands—history, always at least one book of history for flights—and waited as his father conducted some private ritual or sought atonement. Even before security became a sharper presence in such places, Timon's placement and solitude earned him looks, glares from those who wore uniforms emblazoned with some derivative of the word *security*.

Bags checked and metal detection complete, Timon moved down the terminal's crowding corridors toward his gate. He found a cup of coffee and sat down and opened the monograph he carried with him. He had two such volumes, along with a historical dissertation and a pop-science paperback recommended by his father in a way that seemed unavoidable. Timon stared out at the passage of planes and supply trucks across a neutral morning.

The anticipated boarding time arrived with little fanfare. Heads in the waiting area, Timon's among them, turned toward the desk, where a man in a uniform shrugged and apologized. "We don't know yet," he said. "We'll tell you when we know something more." And so Timon waited and read in a sort of stillness. He tried to breathe normally, and yet wondered why airports only held chapels and meeting rooms. Not yet nine in the morning and yet he felt the need to move, whether the space was a crowded bar with busted speakers or a high school's track raised from shredded sneakers. Ninety minutes past the expected boarding call, he surrendered his seat and stood, to walk the terminal for a while. A morning later and three thousand miles to the east, he boarded a train, southbound for Charleston.

The departure from Sea-Tac to New York had been uneventful until the flight's final minutes. A warning came from the pilot: notification of passage through turbulence, a guarantee of bumps, of shudders, of nausea. Timon hated the feel of the drop, that split-second hollowing; his body, all of their bodies falling what would be a fatal distance to them without the jetliner's thin shell. Sometimes there would be screams or involuntary shouts; sometimes Timon would hear groans or grunts from a corner, from a form huddled head to chair, head in hands, hands in prayer.

The storm they'd lurched to clear had rendered delays onto Timon's connecting flight. And so he proceeded to a ticket counter and began to summon demands: demands for a hotel room and a per diem and an early-morning connecting flight. As he spoke he heard his voice and his voice sounded foreign to him, sounded almost childlike, not the low transmission with which he ordered drinks or the hesitant academic's intonation that he found placated certain ebullient clients. This voice, he considered, was not one he wanted recognized as his own. This was the voice of a petulant disgrace.

At first he was shouting; then, thinking better of it, he turned and walked away. Then an elastic return, spinning back and nearly stumbling as he turned, boarding pass in hand. He set it on the counter—gingerly, he thought, be ginger with it—and pushed it slightly toward the attendant. "There's nothing you can do for me?" he asked.

The ticket agent shook her head. "No. If you called the airline, someone there might be able to help. But there's really nothing I can do."

"Then I should just fucking—" He crumpled the ticket, scooped it up. "Fucking get out of here and just...go." He turned and walked off again. Three steps clear of the ticket counter, he recognized himself, reckoned with shame, and spun again. This time he tried not to stumble. The paper sphere sat in his hand, its edges mockingly prodding his skin; for a moment, he wanted it to dig so deep it bled.

Back at the counter. "No, no—seriously? There's nothing you can do." The sad head shake across the counter showing weariness, then panic. "Nothing? So I should just...get in a fucking car and drive to South

Carolina? Will you pay for that? Will you fucking pay for that?" And the heat running through his cheeks, that loss of distinction in his words, his words bleeding into a shout. Timon heard himself elongate the word "God" for far too long. He set down the sphered boarding pass and began to smooth it out, hoping for some sort of restoration. He saw a tabletop pen and saw its flattened edge and began running it over top of the paper, rejuvenation in mind.

From behind him in the line, he heard someone breathe the word "Certifiable." And then the pen was jabbed into the surface through one corner of the board pass, the pen shattered, plastic flaking off into daggers. Then there was an escort for Timon. Repeated again and again: "You should be grateful all we're doing is throwing you out. You should thank God for that." And a low stream of apologies from Timon, not really discernible as such, simply a low mantra of whispered desultory sounds, his head angled into his neck, linoleum floors his epic scenery.

He made arrangements an hour later. A train the following morning, a long slow ride to get him to Charleston. And then a version of his delay, composed for Jonathan Clarligne's ears. Merely a delayed flight, said Timon, a sheepish shift in conveyance. He sat by a hotel room phone and looked out at billboard lights and shifts in the night sky and spoke words that provoked no response from his client save the equivalent of a nod. "So you'll be late," said Jonathan Clarligne. "That can be reconciled."

A taxicab brought Timon to a hotel a handful of blocks from Penn Station. At a restaurant two doors down he ate Korean, waiting for the bowl's heat to sear rice into something crisp and resonant. At the front desk, he made arrangements for an early wake-up call: a six in the morning departure was the critical event of his tomorrow. Four stops on the subway brought him to a clutch of still-open shops, and from them he purchased as much as he could for the following day's transit. The books he bought were large, lavishly illustrated. Documents of cities and scenes and cultures, monographs on artist's works and industrial practices and schematics. And two histories of Baltic nations, his own area of expertise within the business. He knew landmarks, knew the names of cities and avenues; now, he wanted to understand the context in which they dwelled.

Down the street, he found a shop in which he bought a Birthday Party album. After he paid, he stepped across the threshold to the sidewalk and felt the eastern city's air on his face and turned back inside. He added a Born Against album to his purchases and then ventured back to his hotel.

There was a bar a few doors from the hotel's entrance, and once his purchases had been deposited in his room, Timon made his way there, to a stool and a countertop sprawl in front of him. The ale hit the rice in his stomach, and for a moment he remembered his childhood, his parents speaking of throwing rice at weddings and then, a decade later, telling him to avoid this practice, that rice expanded on contact with liquid and tore through avian innards like pencils through a balloon. He felt something quiver in his stomach, a stop-motion shake, and wondered whether this would be where he met his end. Stomach distended and expanded, eventually ruptured from brown ale and bibimbap at an unscheduled point of transfer. Eventually the shakes subsided; Timon lay payment on the bar and navigated the route back to his bed.

Timon's eyes opened; ten seconds later, his alarm began to sound. This was how he woke in hotels: just early enough to outwit the alarm, but not quite early enough to escape its wrath. The shower came in cold, an enemy's shake, an expulsion into clarity. Checkout at the hotel was simple; check-in with Amtrak proceeded gingerly, each participant reluctant to raise their voice. At just after six in the morning, the train departed Penn Station. Timon was alone in first class, his luggage above him and his reading material in the vacant seat beside him. He plugged in his laptop and charged his phone and began his research, the sun still hesitant to cross the horizon.

PART TWO:

SECRET ORIGINS

9

MARIANNE AND ELIAS DROVE north on the interstate. Elias's car was old, its mileage signifying that it was at an age where abandonment would be a reasonable alternative to significant repairs; abandonment or a direct route to the scrap yard. Still, it hummed along, Elias reclining as he drove, the ceiling fabric above Marianne's head beginning to bow. The sky was a sharp shade of blue, a color that seemed to flow into the evergreens flanking the highway rather than demarcating itself from them. Marianne looked ahead, her stare through the windshield mirroring that of Elias. As he drove, Elias's right hand selected a cassette from the console's cubbyhole. *Split Seven Inches*, read the label; Marianne saw it and saw Elias pry it open, withdraw the actual tape from within, and slide it into the stereo. The music began mid-song, a ramshackle acoustic guitar and an untrained voice striving for a higher register.

"Hope you don't mind," Elias said.

"No, it's fine," said Marianne.

The highway ushered them north past Mukilteo and Issaquah toward the night's destination. The cassette moved from grim introspection to long distorted chords and agitprop vocals. From the corner of her eye, Marianne saw Elias's thumb occasionally emulate a rhythm on the steering wheel's edge. Her mouth allowed itself the suggestion of a smile. The sun was at its apex now. "We'll sweat off autumn yet," said Elias. Marianne nodded.

Their destination was an hour or so north. Marianne wondered whether the mountains would look the same from there. The back of the car held gear: a sizable tent, Elias's sleeping bag, and an older one of Marianne's that dated back to her college days. That had earned her the sound of Elias's clicking tongue. "Florida?" he had said. "Shit. That won't serve you well up here. I've got some blankets and an air mattress. You should be okay." There was a cooler: beer and a stray bottle of wine given to Marianne eight months earlier, some food that could be easily roasted. And a container of popcorn, which Elias implied had been added as a joke. "Just like when we were kids," he had said. The gleam in his eye was unexpected. As they passed an exit, Marianne noticed that Elias's glance had flickered in her direction, just for a moment, before returning to its devotion to the road before them.

There was silence for a long stretch of road, mile markers observing a quiet car, its inhabitants' eyes forward, their heads occasionally nodding at a noteworthy site or simply in keeping with the rhythm of their passage. Inside the car, Elias's cassette had come to an end and reversed and started again, its telltale first notes ringing out— except, as Marianne realized, they weren't a demarcated opening to one song but were instead the fleeting coda to the one before it, notes played by a different band entirely.

Elias said, "I'm going to put something new in," and Marianne told him that that would be fine. The tape he chose opened with long ambient clouds, sounds that seemed at odds with the blue and open sky above them. Marianne waited; she was sure she had heard this album before, and knew that if she waited long enough, in would come the drums, and a melody would be born.

Timon watched from the traincar window as it rattled through New Jersey, occasionally sliding past the local train system, the contrast of their motion exhausting him. First class remained empty save him. On the seat beside Timon, their configuration constantly shifting, were his books, his research materials, and his laptop. Though he had tripped through timezones and felt a disconnect from the hour at hand, Timon couldn't sleep. He felt pressed against the outer edge of Eastern Standard Time, body sore as though he had traversed the country's length on his own legs and, having arrived here, was now expected to rest.

He rubbed one cheekbone with the outer ridge of his thumb and felt nothing between bone and skin. He walked to the dining car for his third cup of coffee of the morning, and when he returned he set it before him and his mind began to wander.

When he was seventeen, the family had briefly attended religious services in a cathedral far from any landmarks he could recognize. He recalled a March afternoon in which he had traveled in a car separate from the rest of his family. He remembered a fervor and a lopsided tradition inside, a service which moved from voices near to breaking to a low and minimal chanting of certain select portions of the text. This was a Sunday; on Saturday, his father had brought him into the company's offices in a building downtown. A humble place, he thought, looking on it with eyes different than those of his childhood, when he had been brought here for entertainment rather than prospecting. Then as now, he had looked upon the lines of the walls and their simple adornments and the prints hanging from them and processed. He walked the halls behind his father and his uncle Gilbert, whose presence in these offices at any hour was a given.

Timon surveyed the walls and skipped from image to image, wondering whether the series of images were meant to be an equation, whether the room represented a collage, a riddle for the amusement of the company and no others. Along one wall: maps torn from century-old atlases, grainy photographic prints of rain on cobblestones, and one framed Art Chantry print. He walked and was slowly ushered into the conversation in front of him. Even as he spoke, seeking to impress, most of his thoughts remained on the sequence, running it backward and forward: the meaning of the images as one entered the office and their meaning as one walked from Gilbert's office back to the front door. He would consider this after leaving the office and on the drive back home, and in his own car and down academic hallways for the next few weeks, until a stray remark of his mother's revealed to him that the photographs, the cobblestones gleaming with reflected streetlights, were from Gilbert's camera; that Gilbert walked the city on some evenings, chasing the magic hour; that there was a full darkroom behind some door in the office suite. Gilbert's passion, she said with a smile. And with that, Timon grudgingly surrendered his pursuit of meaning to the sequence. The other images were quantities he could know, but the notion that one of the family could also make art was foreign to him, the revelation of a new letter in a language he had considered familiar, and all of the possibilities that it held.

The polestars—his father, one uncle, and his great-aunt—sat opposite him at the New York office's conference table. It felt unfair. A flash came to him suddenly: standing, younger, classmates advancing on him on the asphalt, knowing he was due a swing and impact and wondering, in those moments between shove and strike, whether they'd draw tears again.

Three from his family sat and looked at him. "This is what we'd like you to study," he heard, and a list was passed to him: dot matrix Courier, shreds of edging straying past the perforation. He looked it over and the admissions process cascaded around him briefly. He looked it over and saw familiarity, concepts and movements that were already more than known to him.

His fingers brushed the surface of the paper, the words' indentations a surprising source of texture. "I know most of this already," he said.

This was greeted with nods. "The degree helps," his great-aunt said. "In certain circles, our methodology, our name, will suffice. Others? Other clients want the right schools, the right names and phrases."

His father cleared his throat and said, "It's a kind of currency." And his uncle said nothing, his gaze skittering from one of the others at the table to the next.

Timon understood his future here, as he looked down at the list. He knew what to say next, swallowed nothing. "Where does it start?" he said.

The next day he arrived at the cathedral in a car, separate from his father. He had been reading about lower frequencies and the way in which they might be brought to resonate throughout the body. It came up in a freeform curriculum he was pursuing, the evolution of his childhood drills. He would wake pre-dawn, take cold showers and coffee, and dwell within ninety minutes of immersion before a typical school day.

The stone building before him seemed ideally suited for resonance, for echoes and arch-echoes. He would search for it that day, in the harmonies sung and the cadences spoken and in their rhythms and call-and-response and clatter. Within the cathedral, he sought his father and grandfather and sat beside them in silence. He waited for a transformation to occur, or at least to begin. Barring that, Timon awaited illumination.

His drive home alone was filled with late-eighties punk rock, surges of guitars and compact rushed harmonies, wordless and buoyant. It brought him a greater sort of comfort. His ritual since becoming a driver ended at the banks of a river, sandwich in hand, watching over a landscape still foreign to him.

A bridge conveyed, the Delaware below, portraits evoking failed connections beside him. The morning still young, Timon rose and walked to the dining car for a fresh cup of coffee.

10

MORNING DRIVES. ELIAS PULLED out a cracked cassette case of an Uncle Tupelo album and fed it to the deck. Morning drives west. Marianne stretched in the passenger seat as best she could, pressing hands to the glovebox and arching her back into padding-foam and auburn-dyed fabric. Morning drives west and Elias cleared his throat and looked to the road ahead. "You all right?" he said.

"I don't camp as much as you," Marianne said, and it was true. The previous night, they had arranged sleeping bags so that they faced one another, rather than laying down in parallel. Elias had been the first to fall to sleep, and quickly began to snore. She ceased the already-dim light in the tent and lay in silence for a while, hoping to find a rhythm in Elias's exhalations.

There had been four circuits of the country before her arrival in Seattle. Four circuits with no false complications;

rather, they had been almost continuous, two grand circles and two treks on the diagonal, week-long sublets and couches surfed and the occasional hostel. Brief jobs and temporary positions that had occupied her time. She had grown to understand the tastes of things in these towns and cities. She could speak with some authority about tap water in Montana and vegetables sold roadside in Alabama, and she found herself feeling a rush of delight on the rare occasions when she saw a statue reflecting some sort of local cryptozoology—a relic of her a childhood fascination with the weird, true, but one that brought a smile to her face even when summoned from memory.

In a Louisville winter, she had met a man named Broder who had undertaken travels similar to hers a few years earlier. He bore tattoos across his body, each one a small memento of the places he had stayed, for good or for bad, that had changed him. Briefly, seated at a bar's booth with three others, she had tallied the cost of them, based on her own brief experience with the process, and wondered how he had managed to afford it. Broder played bass in a series of bands, some of them crude in their chord progressions, others complex in the weave of their melodies with dissonance, and did little else, save for bartending a night a week at the bar in which they regularly sat.

She understood her own economics and had slight inklings of how they might be perceived, of how tenuous they were in certain cities. There had been a few hushed nights of silence awaiting angry or despairing phone calls, hoping for a correct alignment of checks cleared and cashed. The infrequent occasions on which this was required pained her; she felt like someone corseted into the role of compulsive gambler, and when she recalled it after a few years from her space in Seattle, she gladdened herself by noting that it had only been necessary twice, that she had minimized the potential damage done. The shortened breath, the mornings waking with quickened pulse, the nausea that spread throughout those days.

Louisville had been the longest stop on any of the circuits. Long enough to fall into routines and begin to consider places her own; to think about deeper acquaintances and settle in to comforting routines. To consider ending her transit and finding a rhythm specific to this city. She began to consider spaces and neighborhoods and walks, train and bus schedules neglected, "For Sale" signs on cars regarded with interest. Pauses near buildings seeking tenants. Jobs for more than travelers lingered over. A circle began to form, haltingly, of a group of regulars. Which eventually prompted questions on Broder at the waning moment of a night's drinks. Allison was a longtime resident, a friend of the friend who had been Marianne's lodestar in Kentucky. Allison sat in the booth, as did Jeremiah, wispy beard and full-sleeve tattoos. And Marianne turned to them both and posed the question: what was Broder's story? Native or expat, in town for his education or to seek his fortune, local scion or road-borne traveler?

Neither of her friends had known. Broder seemed to them to be some sort of immortal fixture, picking up haphazard bar tabs and occasionally subjecting all in his orbit to fulminations on various topics. A man who could be relied upon for the unanticipated: a display of esoteric knowledge or a quietly crooned song or the revelation of a banjo or conch shell at 3:00 in the morning, then proceeding to chime out a few selections indicating far more than a passing familiarity with its playing. *A charming mammal*, Allison called him. And somewhere along the way, the economics were lost, the conversation led along digressive paths.

When her days in Louisville became languorous, Marianne knew that it was time to leave. Her last days there were a collage: Polaroids of significant places and brief rushes into shops she had come to prize. Items acquired that would feed into a project born in her mind there on a morning where she'd awakened early, the sun still new in the sky. Skills she had formed across the way, skills and predilections and talents. Lost charts she'd vowed to remake. Those were the seeds of her collage, her work in progress that had followed her to Seattle and had traced a route, stops in older cities used as a reason to gather material. Sometimes she'd see a sign of home, of a home, in an odd place: a bar with antiquities and memorabilia for sale on the country's other side, an open-air market that resembled a tent city, an antique volume akimbo on an acquaintance's bookshelf.

As Marianne watched him, Elias wove his knuckles around the steering wheel and sighed. The roads, she noted, had become more organized, suitable for navigation and a certain restraint.

The train crossed the Delaware into Pennsylvania and stopped in Philadelphia and then entered Delaware. The books beside Timon now had placeholders marking their pages, indicating areas of enrichment. Some served as a means for him to expand or revisit things he had believed or sought to believe for over a decade; others would serve as fresh shoots, an expansion of territory, new verses and new expectations. There had been no rhythm to the volumes chosen. Some came at the suggestion of the family, while others were his own acquisitions, some made at random, others intended to fill in gaps between two disparate pursuits which might otherwise have toppled one another, distance mimicking gravity or, more appropriately, magnetism.

Slowly, Timon built his own structures amidst the plans others had blueprinted for him. Areas of his own interest, a burrow-hole where his tallies and disciplines might be brought to serve the purposes of the family, or to serve purposes as yet undefined.

At his university, he had seen a film focused through one character's perspective, in which the ending proved that its protagonist had been in a sort of denial, had cloaked his true motivations and true purposes from all who had watched, the audience included. That this protagonist had, in fact, never been in any danger; that the interrogations he faced pertained not to tangible crimes but to offenses of the soul; that the procedural Timon had thought he was watching was, in fact, something far more metaphysical in its scope.

Timon had felt a sort of betrayal at that, had stormed out of the theater before the final frames faded, then sullenly stalked the green. Timon paced, wearing holes through the grass as though he had been faced with impossible mathematics, with evidence that the calculations he had taken for granted his whole life had suddenly been rendered false. It had happened once before, with the nature of planets; why not now? Why not with anything else?

His grandfather had come to visit him at college in his third semester. By that point, Timon's face had grown lean, his hair slack. His style fit neither the well-off scions he saw daily nor the outsiders in well-worn shirts of an age to have fathered their wearers. He drifted in his own fissures, occasionally carving some of his own. Walks through the campus where he swore he left some sort of trail, an embedded cartography gradually made external.

Timon's routine was notable in its density, his course of study mapped out by relatives in distant cities, always according to the needs of the business. Two majors known for their embedded pressures and a business minor, tacked on for pragmatic reasons. Or so his father had said: "Eventually you'll be needed in the operations, in a financial role." None of the subjects were outside of his areas of knowledge, and he excelled in certain areas and struggled in others. His memory, the facts buried in his mind, his ability to *place*: these were not in doubt. His quality for synthesis—as one professor put it—was more tenuous.

"You should be working toward theories," the professor had said. "You should be seeking a meaning, a method of organization." They sat in a quiet office, the professor's neighbors vanished or silent.

And Timon had felt words form that must be suppressed. *But that's unimportant,* he nearly said before choking them back and learning, in that exchange, to acquiesce with a murmur.

He had taken to ducking in to see music at out-of-the way spaces that had the feel of witches' covens. There were perhaps faces he was coming to know in these collectives, eyes and cheekbones and shapes of chins that were familiar even as they were nameless. He sought a shapeless noise from the speakers, a roar that came in patterns anarchic and brutal, one with a shape he could not anticipate.

It was hard for him to claim the attraction. It began with him a non-drinker, nineteen and withdrawn, an elusive roommate and no habits, nothing that might dissuade him from his work, from pursuits academic and familial. Upon his dispatch to academia, Timon had been told that his work for the business would be reduced to almost nothing. This was not, he was to learn, precisely true. Roughly every six weeks, packets would arrive via post, sometimes brimming with information, sometimes sparse. Affixed were notes and curling facsimile transmissions, ink smudged from their conveyances. Once in a great while there would be transportation somewhere, along with instructions on mannerisms and code of dress. He would scan over photographs and replicated documents stacked neatly between textbooks and notebooks and journals, the last of which found him tracing long routes idly in the night's waning hours, constructing routes that traveled mazelike, complementary to his thoughtpaths for the night. Sometimes his pen dug routes into the page and into the one behind; other evenings found him subtly crossing over the eaves of one page and onto their opposite, his eyes indistinct and his senses muted. If his roommate ever saw Timon engaged in these actions, he never spoke of it.

One night he saw a couple step into a gallery space. One was dressed casually, her shirt silkscreened and readjusted, while the other wore a suit made for a man twenty pounds heavier. Each was beaming. Timon, with no paths in mind, no readings for the night, no business to conduct, followed them inside. Their appearance was a momentary pitch-shift, a short inspiration for Timon's intrigue. There was a discontinuity there, a comfort in how they walked that attracted Timon, a sense that their separation from categorization paralleled his own but achieved something greater, something closer to a standard as yet unnamed.

He followed them in and handed a few dollars to someone collecting at the door. Once inside the room, Timon saw a makeshift stage in one corner, well-worn metal legs and a scuffed surface flanked by two battered speakers. On the stage, places for three players had been set, but only one was used. A man stood there behind a guitar, his look similarly out of time, his face focused on the spaces before him where no one stood, his guitar conjoined to his stomach, his guitar shaken and thrashed as he screamed, his voice hitting peaks and then coaxed itself down. The effect was beautiful and terrifying. The singer declaimed lyrics with wavering syntax, with names and references classical and mythological, roared and cooed. The music's rise and fall collided with Timon and pieced his skin, filled him with the charge of the unknown and the soon-to-be-known.

It could be something of my own, Timon thought two songs later. And the singer made his exit. This could be something of my own. And a band followed the singer, this one four in number, their rhythms more identifiable but their guitar still a howl, their lyrics a jumble, unknown. It struck Timon like a newfound wellspring that offered unconditional bliss.

By the time of his grandfather's arrival in town, Timon had been attending events in unutterable places for several months. He made no friends there; rather, he simply stood and watched as music was played. He imagined that he might see a face familiar from dormitory life or a class, or even a pathway navigated through crowded hallways and elevators even more stifling. He saw none that he recognized, and none gave any indication of knowing him. He would stand midway through the crowd and let the waves of sound reach his anonymity. Timon gorged himself on the sound like a gourmand recently released from prison, and did so as often as he could.

Timon's roommate, a surgeon in embryo, was little seen around their gray-walled alcove. The phone rang one Sunday morning at just after nine. After two rings, Timon took the call and heard his father's voice on the other end. "I'm glad you're up," his father said. "It's a work matter." Poul Ingert, grandfather to Timon, would be making one of his sporadic appearances in the Northeast the following weekend. "Leave your schedule open," Timon's father said.

Poul Ingert lived in Flagstaff at the time, alone in a modest house most of the way up a mountain. He had moved west years before Timon's birth, seeking an atmosphere less taxing on lungs that had, upon the onset of middle age, begun a slow and inexplicable decline. The air in Arizona had rejuvenated him, he told his issue, and isolation had made his mind keener. He appeared as a figure half monastic and half divine, albeit a kind of divinity thousands of years removed: spiteful and arbitrary and, Timon had gleaned from conversations a generation above his own, given to lustful declarations when so moved. Poul Ingert could be relied upon to make short jaunts, fewer than one per season, to visit family and certain valued clients and occasionally and infrequently to deliver lectures. It was the last of these that was to bring him into his grandson's proximity.

"I'm going to send you money," Timon's father said. "Your grandfather will probably pay for the meal, but he's been known to challenge presumptions. He might give you a look when the check comes and refuse all claim on it. You should be prepared." A wad of twenties arrived via carrier two days later, and on the day after that Poul Ingert called Timon about making arrangements for a Saturday lunch.

At first, Timon never knew the names of the bands and artists he saw. Sometimes they would announce it from the stage, and sometimes he would pass a flyer for that night's show, logos pasted together with typewritten descriptions and glued atop a graphic purloined from a comic book, old advertisement, or family photo. Timon stared at these sometimes, attempting to unearth the buried image and assign it to some extant taxonomy.

That night at the space there was motion: the band's drumming attracted a newer, sleeker crowd, a crowd prone to collisions and the clearing of a ovular space in the middle of the venue. Timon saw a nervous look on the face of the man who had taken his five dollars as bodies met bodies frenetically and spun off, the guitars on stage releasing sound that dove through the drumbeat's cut-time rhythm. Some moved with their hands up and reflexively covering their faces and others moved with their hands out, and on the fringes of the space that had been cleared Timon saw others standing back, pushing at those in motion with cross looks on their faces, looks that stopped just short of accusation and indictment. It came time for Timon to dive in. His legs haltingly sought to find a beat to lock themselves to even as he began a circuit of his own.

As he turned, the sense of the music shifted: now the sound from his left ear was overpowering, and as he moved it he felt as though he moved through the crashing chords and drumbeat crescendos like some new style of swimmer. He put his arms up, half in emulation of those around him, and half because he nearly swore he could feel the sounds. It was a feeling not far removed from joy. The music was made tactile around him; it descended onto him; he embraced it, a rush like dreams.

As the band continued to play, Timon began to stretch, began to consider the space around him as the one-two-three-four sped onward, as the notes grew more ragged, as the vocals ten feet from him became more strained, began to ebb. His arms reached out more: he felt the music run through fingers and impact his arms. He imagined it sliding beneath his skin and raising up marks and images and leaving him altered, unrecognizable and redefined. He thought of marathoners observed in the last mile, approaching their contest's end. As he moved, he reached beyond the music's skin and began to push. As he moved, he began to shove and collide, the path toward his own bliss never more certain.

A slow sort of convergence developed in his mind: thoughts of his family, of his work and his learnings and his leavings ushered toward a common center. From the stage, the singer's voice had reached a peak, had shifted past words to a scream from which all comprehension had been sapped. The guitars grew louder, and Timon saw the outskirts of the center, saw the beginnings of an answer.

He reached out for it, not caring what he pushed through now, not concerned with obstacles or boundaries.

And then a hand gripped him by the collar and pulled him away from the space before the band. "Fucker!" a voice not his shouted. "Fucker! You don't do that!" And flung him and prompted stumbling until his momentum brought him to rest at a wall.

Timon woke the next morning red-faced and bruised, informally barred from the gallery that he had come to haunt. It would be years before he stepped inside again, and then only tenuously, paying five dollars for the show and, after five minutes, taking steps away from the massing crowd, toward the door to the outside and then passing through it. The gathered crowd paid him no mind; he drifted away in mock anonymity.

It was nine o'clock on the morning of lunch with his grandfather. The next two hours passed through his hands like tidewater—a rudimentary breakfast, studies conducted below a window as the early day's brightness achieved its mid-day competence. He dressed himself in clothes he still inexorably associated with religious ceremonies and false teenage formality. He resembled someone's idea of himself: an altered, barely recognizable Timon, a semi-formal Timon. At eleven in the morning he walked toward the bus, his route and destination carefully considered, mapped relentlessly.

Lunch was the first time Timon had seen his grandfather in years. His last memory was of a stern face unexpectedly rendered childlike in a cathedral-held mass.

Poul Ingert had been staying with them for a week, but hardly interacted with the children, preferring instead to recount business dealings with Timon's father and bask in the breadth of Timon's mother's knowledge. His was a shape to glimpse through half-cracked doors, an elder making fluid gestures. Timon would watch for a moment and then walk away.

As Timon walked into the restaurant, he felt the return of an old inadequacy, the same sensation that prevented him from lingering outside company conversations in his childhood. He noticed the high ceilings, the columns and their spacing, the minimally placed artwork on distant walls. Brief details about each came to him as he glanced around the room. He saw the diners that populated two-thirds of it. He was clearly the youngest one here; had one of his parents been with him, they would have been just behind him on that list.

Poul Ingert sat alone at a table toward the back of the room, close-cropped white hair making him resemble less a patriarch than an aging agitator, a hidden wrench destined for turning gears or breaking windows. As Timon approached, his grandfather did not stand. Rather, he raised one hand in greeting, palm facing him—a salutation with empires behind it. The hand moved; the greeting became a gesture, indicating to Timon that he should sit.

"I don't see much of you," Timon's grandfather said after pleasantries had been exchanged and food ordered. "Truth is, I don't see much of any of you. I ceded that. I traded it away some years ago and let the others manage the business now. Let a younger generation operate things.

"I'd like to tell you about my own involvement in it. How I came around to the business." To Timon's ears, it sounded like a lecture or a sales pitch. He wondered whether his grandfather had delivered this to each member of his generation in turn: a recruitment and motivational speech all in one. To his knowledge, no one in the family had not been offered a chance to work for the business, and none had left it.

"It was a winter of tangled wires," Poul Ingert began, this confirming Timon's hunches. "I was thirty-nine. Listless and directionless. A bachelor watching his friends' children becoming men and women. I had my Sundays and little else. I taught, in those days. You didn't know that? Your father never told—No. well, wasn't my best work. I wore it like a pudgy man wears a shirt fitted too small for him—that constant inhalation and contortion." He leaned in, jabbing a fork in Timon's direction. "You wrack yourself," he said, then speared a bit of salad.

In that winter of tangled wires, Poul Ingert said, he was at work on a manuscript, one that his apartment encircled like a shrine. In his idle hours, he fancied himself the American answer to Chesterton, and saw this manuscript as a window opened onto this identity. In his idle hours and in relaxed conversations with compatriots, he cited his own ambitions, earning him smirks and facsimiles of respectful responses.

On one night in that selfsame winter, Poul walked down a street, two books under one arm and a wavering hand before him. Snow fell, subtle like dust from a long-untouched volume in some obscure archive. Poul came to a bar and lingered for a moment, the window's signs somehow sirening him inside. If not successful, they at least prompted his lingering beside the window.

As he stood there, a man with oak's build walked outside, stinking of vodka and damp cigars. Poul was pushed aside, and when he regained his composure enough to look at the larger man, he called out. The broad-shouldered man glared at Poul and swung once, then a second time, fists meeting face, leaving Poul unconscious on the street, bruises soon to rise.

When Poul woke, he probed the inside of his mouth with his tongue, proceeding from tooth to tooth meticulously, accounting for the presence of each before he would allow himself to stand. He swore some of the pain before his fall had come from a molar tearing itself from gums and falling outward, blood reaching out as though it hoped to rejoin with his body. But no such thing awaited him on the sidewalk: only his books, opened and sprawling, but still intact.

The night's plans erased, Poul arrived home and tore the bloodied shirt from his body. Buttons whizzed everywhere, ricocheting off bookshelves and, in the case of one particularly determined disc, chiming off the edge of an irregularly stained coffee mug. In the years to follow, Poul would find them in corners, buried beneath rugs and cushions and behind volumes on his shelf, and collect them in a jar, never finding the need to discard them.

Poul surveyed his own form in the mirror, eyes locking into reflected eyes, then encompassing the reddened face, half from blows and half from anger. He thought to himself, You look weak. Reprehensible, a creature to be shamed, mocked, casually struck down by passerby. Not deserving of an explanation or warranting an apology.

Poul walked through other rooms and saw amassed items that seemed alien. They seemed to belong to a previous self, one that required a hasty strangling or smothering. For the items stacked in the rooms outside his study, he quickly found takers, and bonfired the rest. And then he took to the phones, declaiming his dissatisfaction in the hopes that someone might have something, an assignment or position or role more suited to the building of a man less prone to attacks, less prone to contempt. Poul spread notions of his own knowledge and found them receiving receptive ears. In turn, he drew up contracts and worked the late nights of a younger man, venturing into the days on dwindling currents of sleep.

The firm turned a profit from the start. Poul held it in the doorway as a bulwark against the fear and gave thanks to God on Sunday and manufactured fortunes until the tides had gone back to the sea. A year later, he walked with a rigidity in his back; two years from there, it was Poul who inspired fear in others. In him they saw a clenching, a trigger, fingers that could become a fist at a moment's notice.

Timon's grandfather left a pause there, an implied gap into which questions could be asked. A course of food was placed before each of them, and Timon's grandfather tore into it with a younger man's leverage. After half his plate was cleared, after stray crumbs and supple juices had been wiped from his face, he continued.

"I'll tell you of your father now. We made him. We made him smart. We raised him up and set him at the altar most weekends and saw his senses blossom in the classroom. We raised him bright, raised him to know things on instinct. There's a bit of Lamarck in me now, I think." He chuckled, his lips almost spelling out a sentence to follow that, then withdrawing it with a gleam in his eye.

"Then were the years we sent him off to seek his degrees. Sometime between the beatniks and the hippies, he found a way to be worse. Not soft; like a soldier, but fueled by something off its keel. We encouraged him, in those days. We dwindled him and shaped him in the hope that he would emerge into this state of fearlessness as surely as I had. Hoping all the while that he would be ready; your uncle complemented his knowledge well, but never seemed to be the readied heir we needed. Your father? We hoped against hope we might see him operate the firm one day. And we spent years doubting that anticipation.

"I know. Your father. You never saw him as a child, never saw him indecisive. Never saw him scared. One late-night call, him to me, his voice shaking. He'd botched something. His voice shook. What it was, I couldn't say. It was an obstacle. It was something that could be repaired, as he needed to be repaired. As he shook and quavered and stumbled before us, we sought to restore him. At fifteen, your father was a god; the potential he had made all of us shake. And when we saw him at nineteen, at twenty, how we grieved.

"We sought restoration. We drew him to us after his commencement. We dredged forth the beneficial parts and culled out the ones that were damaged, before their rot could spread. A sort of moral gangrene that was stripped away.

"There were years that he strayed again, and then your father became devout. Far more than me. Far more than my wife or my sister, than his brother, than anyone. We thought, for a brief period, we might lose him to a monastery or the priesthood. We had words; we spoke with him. We convinced him of his value to us, strengthened our tithe, ameliorated his vows.

Poul Ingert's face grew softer. "It was a beautiful time," he said.

Timon cleared his throat. "I didn't ever know that," he said.

His grandfather smiled. "I wouldn't expect your father to ever speak of it. Or acknowledge it, truth be told. It was never his finest moment." He angled his glass toward his grandson. "I wonder of your devotion, Timon. And I can only say this: it's a stronger place, where your father and I dwell. A strength that our faith gives us, and a kind of balance. A sense of restoration. A surefootedness. No stumbling or being attacked or assailed. You don't flail in the darkness. You might doubt, Timon, but you do so without the fear."

Over their coffee, Poul and Timon spoke of Timon's planned work with the firm over the summer. No more family history was unveiled before the younger man's eyes, and no details of Timon's life here were demanded of him. They parted with a handshake, Poul toward his hotel and Timon toward the city bus, the fare in his hand and a coastal geography taking shape in his mind. The summer would take him elsewhere, would take him to a quiet office maintained by some distant relation, annexed to the firm a half-decade before. The summer would envelop him in the firm's business and would impart to him grim tidings of knowledge and a sense of affairs and decorum. As he sat nights in an upscale city's subleased apartment. His furnishings spartan, his meals in monochrome, he anticipated his work in the firm until that anticipation became something else, something like an upended form of dread. It was then that he began a consideration of coastlines beyond the one he had known since birth; it was then, his eyes darting across maps, that he pondered his own relocation amidst the sound of guitars.

11

MARIANNE AND ELIAS FACED a locked door at the tattoo shop at one in the afternoon. The door's sign listed an opening time thirty minutes earlier. They had passed a sandwich shop less than a mile the way they'd come, Elias saying, "We need to go there afterward. I'll be famished," and Marianne allowing herself one subtle cringe. Here they were, on time and eyeing the road's lines for a figure bearing linework. The only number Elias had been given was for the shop's own countertop phone, something they learned when they dialed it and—faintly at first, then with the clarity of recognition—audited its trill as it sounded from the other side of thin glass.

The parking lot sky was a welcoming gray—not the haze that gives way to a humid sun or the massed shapes that give way to cloudbursts, but something promising wind and languor. This was the sort of color you could gather round you and dwell in, even if only briefly. A transitory neutral shade, a traveler's friend, made for silhouettes and portraiture.

Their drive from the campsite had been jocular, Marianne thought. No eager glances from Elias toward her, either in the car or as they'd sat at breakfast in a diner near Issaquah. Instead, she found herself talking about her project, about assemblage and mediation, about allowing two images or objects to interact, even if only for a moment, and to see whether they clashed or agreed, could become conjoined or would stand at odds. Elias listened, enraptured, only breaking gaze with her when idly surveying his text's future home.

Two storefronts down from where they waited was a doughnut shop. There, caffeine and sugar, in varied forms, were purchased to aid in their observance. They stood beside Elias's truck, Marianne in sunglasses. A car pulled up one stop away—not their quarry—and provided a surface for reflection. "We look like a band," Elias said with a smile. The remark dwindled down and suddenly became a jab halfway through Marianne's digestion. She wondered whether that was subconscious shorthand, whether Elias was in fact telling her that she looked aloof. In this scenario, Elias would be the drummer, she knew. In his mind, Elias would always the drummer: steady and half-obscured, the cast of his eyes forever excused.

Marianne took a bitter shot of coffee and took her turn at observance. Not a band, she thought. They looked like miscast actors, playing sullen teens in someone's off-brand melodrama. Each of them in a role their junior by the better part of a decade. At that moment, she wanted a shower and a familiar view. She looked over at Elias and smiled. "How long do you think we should wait?" she said.

Timon's train took him south, through Washington and down tree-lined tracks that defied a geographic placement. He felt separate from any maps now, displaced as though he had been taken surgically from a city's surface and mounted below glass, a subject for scientific classification. On the train, eight hours down, he shivered. A hole in his stomach asserted itself, prompting still more shakes. It was an old friend come back after long absence, a hearty handshake and a wicked gleam in the eye. An unwelcome guest, this old fear, this nervous fit. This transient discomfort, cloaking Timon, not ill-fitting, not like shrouds fitted for an older body. Not a childish cloak at all.

Two thirty, he thought. Two-thirty was fine for a drink while in transit. He walked to the bar car and purchased a beer and took it back to his seat. Sat and watched the books beside him. Opened one and sought photographs of a community, a right and proper scene. He saw kinetic images and arcs in the air, a photographer's flash echoed in the downward motion of a guitar, its player here anonymous, face blurred, T-shirt unreadable. He saw tours in thumbnail, saw studio sessions and apartments and well-worn practice spaces. Timon closed the book and opened another, brushing up on areas of knowledge useful to the family business. It drifted into him and his knowledge of the sounds of motion bled out. Four hours to Charleston, he thought.

Elias drove toward Seattle, no wordplay inscribed on his arm. Marianne watched him. They had stood beside the car for five hours, waiting for the shop's neon OPEN to become lit from within, hoping for the existence of a back entrance through which some artist might have slipped. Two hours into watching, a light rain had begun to fall, and they had taken shelter inside the car, occasionally making runs to a deli a few storefronts down for supplies: first water and then, after some debate, a pair of pre-fab sandwiches (Swiss cheese, lunchroom turkey) that left them unmoved. Eventually, Marianne had offered to run down to a nearby pay phone and call the number stenciled on the tattoo shop's door in case someone might have slipped inside. The phone had rung and rung, with no machine or human voice providing an answer. Three such calls had she made before, by mutual consent, the decision was made to return home.

Elias had a sour look on his face, a stubbled variant on a child deprived of a favorite toy. On the interstate, after they'd passed a familiar exit, Marianne looked at him. Elias deserved a better weekend than this, she thought, even with her reservations about his choice of tattoo. She thought about salvage. "Dinner?" she said after a while. "I have things at home; I could call Esteban and Iris."

He looked up, an eager light in his eyes. "Sure," he said. "I wouldn't mind, you know, showering first, but—

that sounds wonderful." Marianne saw him twitch slightly after the last word's enthusiasm.

He dropped her off in front of her apartment in the late afternoon's pale sunlight. Three hours later, he arrived again, washed and cleaned; his bones, no longer shrouded by stubble, leaning through his skin. Marianne was talking with Esteban and Iris when he arrived, their conversation, as always, about art and the mechanics of small business loans. It was a good dinner, the four of them splitting three bottles of red wine and making headway through a fourth, this one of port. Of them, the largest share by far was taken in by Elias, and he was also the first to depart, bidding farewell at ten-fifteen after asking Marianne whether he could pick his car up the following day.

Iris and Esteban stayed around for another hour before quietly bidding Marianne farewell. She made herself a cup of tea and sat in the apartment, the sounds of cars passing and a few hardy Sunday night drinkers drifting in slowly, as though the soundwaves they had birthed wanted to savor the night air for a while before reaching windows and drifting through.

Marianne stood and opened each window wider. She took two deep draughts of tea and twisted her head slowly.

At the deli near the tattoo shop, she had bought a road map of the state, had slipped it into her back pocket before rejoining Elias in the car. She hadn't understood the impulse as she did it; rather, she had understood on some level that it represented a new project, a work separate from her primary cartography, but had not yet given the specifics a definite form. Now it came to her; she produced the map and laid it on the worn and spattered work-table she used for drafting. In one closet was a spare board, purchased for use as a shelf but decommissioned; this, too, she took and set on the table. On a ledge in the same closet was an adhesive; in a drawer, a knife for the cutting and a mat to layer atop the table.

In a Belltown apartment, Marianne began the work of excising the weekend's route, her mind already rearranging arranging interstates and local highways, their destination presently a null set, the stakes anything but small.

PART THREE:

FULL ON NIGHT

12

TIMON HAD EXPECTED A driver to meet him when he stepped off the train into a humid Charleston night. Instead, Jonathan Clarligne stood outside the low-slung station, an impeccable figure, miraculously free of palpable sweat. Timon paused a body's length from Clarligne as Clarligne looked him over—a steady procession from shoes to face. "Your train's late," Clarligne said.

"Not my fault," said Timon.

"No," said Clarligne, and beckoned him toward the car. After the luggage had been placed inside and the two men had taken their seats, he continued. "We've got you in a hotel near the old town. I don't expect you'll need a car for the trip. Everything's walkable." He cycled his fingers down the steering wheel. "Should be just like home."

Headlights were subsumed within a humid haze as they drove. Timon wanted a meal and he wanted to see

Clarligne's pictures again: the shotgun, the preacher; wanted to sift through to see patterns beneath the surface. He craved that moment of connection the way epicures crave new tastes, the way lovers starve for a certain touch. Clarligne wore a light blazer over a silk shirt that looked untouched by the air's moisture or the body's means of cooling. Timon looked over at him and felt rumpled, unformed; his lack of sleep blindsided him and summoned him toward rest.

"There's people here you should meet," Clarligne said. "There's a small restaurant at your hotel. I've arranged something."

"I appreciate it, but—"

"You're on our clock now, Timon. Plenty of time on the train to sleep, if you'd needed it then. This will take an hour, at most. Should you need stimulants, we have stimulants."

"Coffee sounds good." It was a compromise, Timon thought, that he could live with.

"I'm not talking about coffee." The look that came into Clarligne's eyes at that moment reminded Timon of his client's youth. It was a look that his father had warned him about. *The look of a life without consequence*, his father had said. *When you see that look, that's your cue to decide whether or not you want to walk.*

Timon coughed. "We'll see," he said. "When we get to the hotel."

Dinner was caterer's generic: carrots and broccoli cooked with a slight tinge of butter and little else, chicken roasted

in a way that bled from it all notable qualities, and a
dollop of onions caramelized at an echelon leagues above
the course's other components. A line-cook savant back
there, Timon thought. He had hoped that the attendees at
this dinner would be relevant to the process he planned to
undertake while here. Instead, they were Clarligne's fellow
scions: gleaming with unknown pleasures and flush with
loose money. He doled out business cards at Jonathan
Clarligne's request, a dispensary for theoretical expertise.
He stifled yawns with the help of whiskey's sharpness and
pungent shivers.

Clarligne bid him farewell just after eleven. Clarligne
and his peers had designs on a nightclub downtown, were
traveling there en masse. An invitation was extended to
Timon, and that invitation was declined. Instead, Timon
waited until his client was out of sight and crossed to the
front desk. He asked about alt-weeklies and requested
a neighborhood map. If he was to be here for a week
or more, ensconced in a hotel friendly to a pedestrian
traversal of the city, the least he could do would be to seek
some localized oblivion.

Timon's hotel room seemed constructed for neutrality:
the walls an off-white color, the furniture representative
of no specific period. He set his suitcase and his traveling
bag on the edge of the bed and began a thudding transfer
of clothing from both into the dresser before him. On
the walls, a pair of pastel landscapes framed in gold leaf
punctuated a view of nothing in particular. The paintings'
view was of a world gone blurred, a vista taken in by an

observer lacking corrective lenses. This was how the room seemed to Timon—not by virtue of drink or anything similar, but via simple fatigue. When he had finished with his clothing, Timon arranged reference works and files around the space. He found himself standing stock-still then stumbling forward, his movements hazy, perception drifting. In his last conscious moments, he scrawled a note to himself laying out the following day's objective: to see the site housing Clarligne's photographs. From there, the project hung vaguely open, offering ambivalent promises.

The morning Marianne got good news from Iris and Esteban was the same morning Marianne got bad news from Archer. That morning was one punctuated by thunderclaps, hurried in their arrival as though behind schedule and rushing toward an engagement somewhere nearer Spokane.

The Clarligne project hadn't gone through, Archer told her. He side-stepped into her office looking dismal, some blood on his cheek suggesting difficulties while shaving. "Foppish fuck doesn't want us involved anymore," Archer said. "Sounded almost apologetic when he talked to me." He shrugged, dark circles below his eyes and an extra week's worth of hair jutting out from his skull. Marianne considered his distress: personal or business? And if it was the latter, should his distress be hers as well?

Marianne suggested that he shut the door, but Archer shrugged. "I've got no hesitation about calling a man out for his foppishness," he said, then slapped the doorframe.

Archer winced, rubbing an apparently injured finger across his lower lip. "This is a piss-pot of a day," he said.

Marianne idly tapped a knuckle on her desk's taut surface. "Anything that should concern me?" she said. Archer shielded his eyes and shook his head.

"No," he said. "Honestly, this is mostly a relief. Would've been extra work, would've stretched us more than I'd have liked." His laugh was a death rattle, a summoning of some awful sound meant to reassure. He squinted one eye, then tilted his head like a dog in the presence of a teakettle. "If you hear from that guy again," he said, "put him through to me. I think we need to have words. Still." He cleared his throat, and continued. "Even now."

Word reached her a few hours later that a grant had come through for Iris and Esteban's pet project. Marianne left the office at seven that night and sat with them at an immaculate bar where drinks were forged at the countertop, ingredients mashed and swirled and decanted. Toasts were offered and plans made; schedules charted and contingencies recounted. It was in this discussion that Dana Guterson's name was raised—specifically, by Esteban, as a patron or subject of the museum. "Funny," said Marianne.

Why "funny" was the obvious question, and was posed as such.

"For a while, I was trying to get ahold of her. Some piece of art of hers; I was trying to figure out if someone in it was someone I'd seen around town."

Esteban chuckled, leaned in with the confidence of an empty stomach and bourbon. "A paramour?"

"Fuck no," she said, and the harshness of it grated even her own ears. "More like—someone to dissect. To try to figure out what makes a bad man bad." She paused, fatigued, correct words elusive. "Not bad, necessarily. Inexplicable would be the best word to use."

"I noticed you were using the past tense," said Iris.

Marianne nodded. "You can only spend so much time on that kind of thing," she said. "I have other things in mind now. I'd rather translate my own mind than look for piecemeal accounts of someone else's. If I see the guy's face around town, I see his face around town. Or not."

13

Jonathan Clarligne had left keys for Timon at the hotel's front desk. A warehouse, eight blocks away, was the destination; still standing empty after the photographs had been found. Timon ate a terse breakfast and set out into the day wearing the lightest attire he could find. It still wouldn't be sufficient, he knew, to keep the sweat away. He would need something softer, something with space, not the long sleeved shirts and densely woven jeans his working methods favored.

He took a to go cup of coffee with him, and was drinking it as he stepped through the hotel doors into the air outside. It seemed to him as though it was aiding him in reaching a state of equilibrium with the sidewalk air, the moisture brutalist as it bore down on him. Nine in the morning: Timon watched people go by in their suits, unfazed by the climate. It left him mystified. Through the glass doors, he heard the hotel's phone ringing, heard the muffled sound of a pickup, a breezy welcoming voice, the words left behind as they translated through cracks into the open world.

Timon walked down clean sidewalks, amidst emissaries of a region unknown to him. The coffee dug down his throat and disoriented his stomach. He wondered if word of his misbegotten travel had reached his father yet, if he should expect a call during his Carolinian foray. Wondered whether he should expect a visit during this time, whether his standing would be in jeopardy. As far as he knew, positions in the family business were inviolate, intact short of resignation or death. Certain nights he feared a summoning back to New York, feared family dinners turning to talk of redundancies, feared his own position becoming a liability. Nine in the morning and this line of thought made him want some sort of obviation, in work or sound or sting.

Call his father, then. Preempt the bad news. The soft sell; formulate a reason for the trip by train. Formulate a reason for the exception to his normally rational methods of travel. Elide away notions that this might be getting worse; filter out the concept that you might be evolving into something unreliable. They'll bring you back into the fold, he thought. Back to the cathedral. A semblance of conviction until it becomes more than a semblance. An automation of belief.

Although, he asked himself, isn't that already what you're doing? He hastened his pace, sweatstains and shortness of breath carried along with him, trotting just below the reach of his hands.

Obstructions within the windows' glass—old paint and dirt smears—were what made the warehouse bearable in daylight. Could it even be considered at a different hour? Certainly at nighttime, lit from within—but any light fixtures mounted to walls or ceiling beams were by now antiquated and unreliable, gutted, or obsolete. The paint that had endured was white, and the structure itself was a light gray; had the windows been opened, had the sunlight been given full license to flow, all that Timon now saw would be washed out with light, would bring tears to eyes and heaviness to lids. The face of God in a warehouse in Charleston, he thought, and grew a hollow grin.

There was a hole in one wall; Clarligne had left copies of the photographs there. Timon withdrew them, shuffled them in his hand, resisted the urge to give them a narrative. The indications of a wedding, the Prohibition-era child with firearm, the formal man with a gutted sleeve below a tuxedo jacket. Find the shotgun, Clarligne had told him. He was here to find the shotgun, and nothing more.

And yet: the room, flooded with light. Timon withdrew into himself: a compensation. A disappearance into memory. The child, now a bishop: a bootlegger's son. The photographs: all from the same camera, taken over the course of a decade or more. The wedding? Incidental. He heard wind pick up outside. The glare coming through the windows lessened.

Two public questions and one private one remained. The private one: the question of the torn sleeve. Animal attack? Dog or cat? Did they have predators here in the Carolinas, Timon wondered. Mountain lions, wolves, or wild dogs. He had no doubt that the photographs had been taken somewhere close to this space. Even with the lack of landscapes, telltale background details, historical figures, or landmarks. He could label it, wanted to label it, wanted pen and ink and adhesive for application. Six photographs, he would inscribe, taken between 1923 and 1942 in Charleston, South Carolina. Other images he had seen dangled in his mind around these and reached toward them. Other images that matched via make and model of camera or mode of clothing or years. He could walk, could carry these with him; could pull body apart and leave a museum revealed.

He began to walk the warehouse's floor. He began to notice the walls: some intact, some pried apart by crowbars and handheld hammers set to clawing. The assumption, as yet unconfirmed by the word of Jonathan Clarligne: the photographs, found by workers dismantling the building. The images deemed scandalous: a bishop, ruined in life or prescreened for posthumous disgrace. The images handed off to Timon for discretion: his own and his family's business, their reputation. Timon's feet seemed to sink into the old floorboards, the wood underfoot not creaking but simply seething, exhaling like something massive, the stomach of some leviathan. He breathed in and out as he turned his head, charting the process of the room's demolition. Four hundred feet, end to end.

The efforts to dismantle the walls had ended a third of the way through with a jagged line that ended halfway down one of them. Upon finding the photographs, the process had ended immediately. A scandal. Quash the scandal, then. Beckon young Timon to Charleston, beachhead and filter.

One public question: the shotgun's location. Timon walked to the wall and began to tap. Clearly, it wouldn't be this easy, but still. He struck the walls at short intervals: hollow all the way around. After one circuit had been completed, he struck the wall again just to hear how the sound traveled. To hear whether the back wall produced an echo. To stand before the resonance and allow the resonance to seep into his skin. His shirt, Timon noted, was dry.

No sounds came from outside. Whoever had built this place, Timon thought, had built it sturdy, had made it isolated. He looked at the beams in the ceiling, at the structure surrounding him. He considered years. He cleared his throat and set the photographs down on an improvised table close to one of the desiccated walls. He opened the front door and locked it behind him, then crossed the street and stared at the building's shell. He chose new vantage points, making circuit after circuit of the warehouse from outside. Cars passed and the occasional pedestrian stared at Timon's observation. He continued his walk, calculating, making comparisons.

Best estimate: put the warehouse in the late 1930s, early 1940s. Photographs, then, placed there after the fact.

He crossed the street, re-entering the warehouse. The door hung open behind him as he walked to the jagged edge of the demolition. The tear in the wall ended at shoulder level. He looked at the paint, the age of the wood, taking in the abbreviated arc made by the act of tearing into the structure. He sniffed it, then crossed the room to the other side, seeking an intact wall. The paint seemed off: more recent, a more nuanced shade. He circuited the room again and again, marking where different sections had been repainted. By four in the evening, his work there was done. Taking the photographs with him, he made his way back to the hotel.

The first call that he made was to his father. A short message was left, hopefully cordial, summarizing his trip so far and leaving the hotel's name and number. The second was to Jonathan Clarligne. This, too, resulted in a message being left—specifically, a request to meet to discuss his findings. Timon hung up the phone and poured himself a glass of water. He opened the alt-weekly and held the city map beside it, hoping to formulate a plan for the night.

Twenty minutes later, Clarligne called back, setting a meeting for that night at a bar fifteen blocks away, a rooftop affair, a name unfamiliar to Timon from the afternoon's research. He returned to his papers, hoping to calculate a newfound plan for the night once his conversation with Clarligne had ended. Nothing came to mind, though—

no dive bars or punk shows to be found, no places where noise might overwhelm him.

Before he walked to the meeting point, he took out a notepad and summarized the day's findings in shorthand. He changed his shirt, toweled off his face, and readied himself for the evening's conversation.

Jonathan Clarligne sat alone at a table on a downtown bar's roof deck. Before him was a drink, ebbed into, clear, ice-filled. Timon wagered vodka. He ordered whiskey at the bar and settled in across from his client. Clarligne hmphed and raised his glass in a halfhearted toast, returned by Timon. Timon cleared his throat after taking an abbreviated drink from his glass. "So," he said. "I've been through the warehouse. I've got a sense of the timeline here, and I have a pretty good idea of where the shotgun is not."

"Good," Clarligne said.

"I assume talking to the bishop himself is out of the question?"

"You assume correctly."

Timon nodded. "Is there anything else I need to know right now? Charleston isn't the largest city I've had to do this kind of work in, but neither is it the smallest."

Clarligne smiled. "Stop by our offices tomorrow. I think we can move to verification."

This paused Timon in the act of raising glass to lips. "Why bring me out here, then?"

"An antique shotgun is still a shotgun," Clarligne said. "Not the easiest of objects to ship. The cost of shipping a man from Seattle to Charleston was significantly less than shipping a trio of firearms to the Northwest."

Timon considered the glass before him. He twisted it, as though trying to wrench a hole through the table. "What does the bishop make of all this?"

Clarligne smiled. "The bishop is quite grateful for the process," he said. "And he'll be even more satisfied when it's been finished." He completed his vodka and bid Timon good night.

Timon sat there for a time, eyeing the remainder of his bourbon and pondering a second drink. When he stood, his thoughts on an abbreviated dinner, he realized he understood the nature of the arrangement now, and wanted nothing more than to be finished in Charleston. Nerves brought salt moisture bundling on his brow; Timon grabbed at a napkin from the bar for blotting as he made his exit.

He found a bar to settle into, brick-walled and anonymous. He had a beer, then had a second. He did not seek dancing, nor did he wander north or south in search of something more kinetic, the impact of bodies on bodies and its jarring absolution. After his third beer in as many hours, he returned to his hotel and stood in the gray scale room. He noticed a flashing light on the telephone. He dialed in, wondering which camp the message had come from. Fewer than ten knew of his presence here, after all.

There had been a brief time in Seattle when he had had a proper social circle. Through a college friend or two, he had briefly been a friend to some who lived there. Had

established a calm in which he could dwell. Groups of four
or five, afternoon drinks or brunches on a rainy weekend
morning. Bars at which he was a subdued regular. The
occasional house party, a time when he could appreciate
music as music, not simply as trigger or incentive. A
time, he thought, when his work would take him out of
Seattle for a week and there would be people waiting to
greet him upon his return. Once or twice, he'd even sent
postcards—a Santa Fé trip he recalled with perfect clarity,
and a shorter one to Halifax.

Even now, he could not precisely demarcate the point
at which he became solitary, though he could recognize
that there had been a general bleeding away of those
around him. There had been a cooling—he did remember
that, and it squatted like an imp in his memories, a fierce
border between states. A point after which calls were no
longer returned, a region of awkward pleasantries and
pleasantries gone blurred from alcohol and fatigue. It had
not, he had come to realize, coincided with the end of his
relationship with Dana Guterson—a breakup that, while
not entirely amicable, was also not horrific, a case study
that peers might cite when ending their own relationships
to say, "Well, at least it never got that bad." But the
breakup had accelerated things, sped up certain processes
toward inevitability.

Seattle felt empty. A return to it from Charleston
seemed as arbitrary to him as a return to Princeton or
New York or his college haunts. There were visitations to
his onetime bars, but he recognized neither patrons nor

tenders. There were periodic nights when, hungry and wandering, he found himself striding down previously familiar sidewalks, looking across the street at buildings that had once held meaning for him. Jonesing his own history for a different city, an improbable one where he might be welcomed home again.

The message played. His father. A quiet inquiry as to how his work was proceeding. Nothing significant: quiet, awkward pleasantries—the reduced shape of most of their exchanges in recent years. Timon was unsure of whether it even warranted a response. The dispatch, the relay, the inevitable tithe, and the return home. A guaranteed routine, an enclosure. City's darkness around him, Timon wondered if he could even function outside the company's sphere, and pondered, in alternating arguments, a rambling life and a return to the fold.

14

HERE WAS A WOOD block compass that Marianne had carried with her since her time in Texas. Two days before finishing most of the work on the introductory map, she had purchased a small canister of light gray paint on her way home from work. She immersed the surface of the wood in this paint, then withdrew it and let the excess fall away. When paint was taut over surface, she brought it above the smaller map—a collage, layers of years' worth of maps, contemporary and historical, certain paths gouged out and altered, newspaper photos xeroxed and colored in by hand—and placed it, pushing down with an even pressure. Her seal, she thought, and pulled the wood block away, leaving the navigation on her ersatz chart forever set.

It was ten-fifteen and she felt a craving for air. Leaving the piece stabilized, she walked down the steps to the street below. It was a Thursday night, and quiet. From another street, she could hear cars in transit, ghost drives propelling themselves from block to block, fading before she could consider them in full.

There were things she considered saying. It was a late enough hour that friends who might be reasonable recipients of those words would be turning in for the night, would not welcome a transmission from her apartment to theirs. An inefficiency, a collapse. More lost words, to be dispersed into air or—if the fit was correct—subsumed into her larger atlas. But words carved or typed onto a stable surface would not restore this night's hollowness; that was a deferred fix, an installment-plan cure for solitude, patchwork and unsteady on its feet.

In the end, she went to a bar and sat alone, hoping to avoid awkward conversation and running two, three, four versions of how that might go in her head. The rye she drank went down quickly, and she did not order a second. Aside from the usual pleasantries with the bartender—not someone she knew—she spoke a total of five words in her half hour there. From there, home, words unsaid to an undetermined partner still hanging, precariously, in mid-air.

Walking toward the morning's meeting with Jonathan Clarligne, it struck Timon that he had not called his father back. The air around him sputtered rain like saliva born from an agitator's spiel. He ducked his head, no umbrella in hand, and again checked the address scrawled in smudged pencil on hotel stationary. His client had promised clarification: three shotguns there to verify.

Three possibilities; one might be correct, or none of them would be the end of this particular search.

He could leave Charleston that night, he realized. Rebook his flight or take a slow train home. Banter and barter in dining cars and sleeping cars, attempt to reconnect with the world, detach himself from observation, usher himself slowly toward something that might, at some future point, become a home.

As he walked, Timon thought about how he might reconcile himself with greater Seattle. There were, he knew, a few of his old friends with whom he might possibly reconnect. True, there was alienation there: a wall of static and silence, of correspondence not responded to and messages left unreturned. He thought about clear nights, wandering the city sober and only slightly less than sober, scratching a nostalgic itch, briefly hoping for a space to be as it was, for a chance meeting to be replayed in the way it had been in his early days living there. The replays never came, and Timon returned home to curse his own impulses or to a bar to submerge them, to keep them stifled below a certain level. To leave his blinders on, to blunt the aches and stings brought by his own history.

Reconciliation. Or something more, some new community. The family had joked to him about his becoming a churchgoer; his sister Kiasma having met a boyfriend there, a boyfriend to whom she was now affianced. Timon had huffed about it at the time and since then; he did not expect to be invited to the wedding, and if he was he was likely to send his regrets, citing distance or inventing a conflicting event.

As Timon walked, he noted one hand clench and expand. He momentarily envied the believers in his family for that window into a community that they had. It would not be his, he knew, could not be his, but it seemed to him to be a shortcut. Others had their art, their work, their children, their academic lives, their hobbies, their pursuits, their families, their craft. He had nothing but the dissection of time and his own ramblings, the fitful walks through neighborhoods in Seattle preceded by fitful walks through his college town and stabler walks, no less fraught with doubt, through the streets around his home. In those moments, he would bleed if only to summon a trickling balm.

He checked the address on the sheet of hotel stationary with the oaken door before him and found a match. Set flesh to wrought-iron and knocked, and, soon after, was granted entry. The room into which he walked was white-walled and washed out, blanched stones inset into surfaces, lending it a patchwork austerity. Timon was directed down a hallway. He could hear coughing from the room he assumed to be his destination. As he walked, he saw more inset stones and wanted to run his fingers over them, to gouge knuckles into them and leave traces of himself there, a signpost, an offering, some sort of ritual to clear himself of these thoughts.

The lamp-lit room into which Timon walked was stark: a simple desk, a few folding chairs, long-buried floorboards newly disinterred. Jonathan Clarligne sat in one of the chairs clearing his throat; before him on the table rested three firearms. At first, they looked identical, and Timon stepped closer to the table to begin immersing himself in their differences. Each was contained in a large and anonymous clear plastic bag.

"I'd like histories," Timon said. He was nodding, he realized. Nodding before he'd even finished speaking, looking down at Clarligne as though he had any right to condescend. Stop it, Timon told himself. He wanted, at that moment, to pull himself into Clarligne's skull, to run a tap through the thoughts that traveled in his client's head, to see how he might appear to others. Were his own conceived notions of a well-dressed man rooted in fact? Was he compelling, or merely competent? Timon stood there, collars and cufflinks jutting from jacket sleeves, no tie in this heat, a few tell-tale indicators of sweat beginning to blossom on his chest. Jonathan Clarligne cleared his throat, then raised one hand palm to the table.

Jonathan Clarligne nodded methodically, his motion controlled like a dancer's, and he reached into his jacket. For a moment Timon's mind took him to cliche, envisioned Clarligne pulling out a minute revolver and shooting once, twice, leaving Timon's body prone and sweating blood on the floor beside the table. Another abandoned room, this one housing a body, housing three sealed firearms. Not the perfect crime, Timon thought, but something close to it. A thesis project in a perfect-crime master class. And then something sensible rose in him and overwrote the accumulated paranoia. No more horrors for this morning, he told himself. Temper the arched curves and coils that wrenched up his back and neck. Breathe, he told himself.

Clarligne handed a trio of index cards up to Timon. Each looked hand-typed, and Timon couldn't resist the urge to hold each in turn up to the light, to savor the canyons made from typescript, to stare at each one and then gaze at the air a foot from his eyes and then, after most of a minute, to silently conclude that each had been issued from the same typewriter, to picture that typewriter in turn and offer a silent guess as to its vintage. Let Clarligne stare, he thought. This is mine.

Three biographies of three weapons. Clarligne's voice: "This is to avoid scandal. The bishop? He knows we're working, but doesn't know it's come this far." Three histories: where the guns had been made, and more generally, for how long they had been in circulation; notable histories, notable facts. Cheat-sheets meant to trigger associations in his mind. This was how Timon operated: not entirely in the manner of his father and grandfather. A subconscious business, his father had called it once during better days. "It's a funny thing," said Clarligne. "I'm still not sure why your father recommended you for this when half your family would have been closer."

Timon coughed, punctuation for his fugue. He had a feeling he knew why. "A kind of education, is my guess," he said faintly. "My father's big on lessons. Even now." From the corner of one eye, he saw Clarligne subtly nod. Timon found himself walking to an isolated part of the room, then stopping, then walking back to the table. He felt wholly tactile, fingers running over fingers and craving something more, craving perception, becoming tools waiting at the ready. He looked at the first gun, picked it up, held its barrel close to his eyes, holding it close so that he might not see the plastic hovering around it. He looked over its surface for artifacts even as he knew that the possibility of artifacts was low, that there would be no crucial detail shouting out its story, that his solution would come from gouges and scuff marks, from smudges and lovingly smoothed patches, from indicators and quirks and quiet tells. He considered the gun and moved on to the next.

For Marianne, the Seattle days were passing like summer storms. There was work during the days and atlas construction at night, and periodic visits to the space soon to be filled with Iris and Esteban's small museum. Those were nights of sheet-rock and drywall and, later, the staining of wood, aided and concluded by red wine. Their hands the next day bore a rare and unique mottling, never repeated. At times it would be severe enough to occasion a comment at work or a bartender's odd look.

Elias was drifting, she heard from a mutual friend. Keeping to himself, amassing more tattoos, occasionally visible in the background at a rock show or wandering out of a bar just before last call. Marianne remembered something he had told her once: "I never like being the last one out," he had said. "I always stay just sober enough to mind the time. Fifteen minutes before I know they're going to say it, I down my last, I settle up, I walk outside. I always hate being the one to force something awkward." It might simply have been Elias's time to wander, she thought. That was the sort of creature their group was: shifts, a dance, roles to be filled, comfort offered and, sometimes, comfort given.

Then there was the case of her own work: the map of the road trip complete, waiting to be shown to Iris. Iris's request to her delivered with grave clarity, hands coming to rest on shoulder blades: "Show it to me. Not now, but soon." Marianne had never before thought Iris capable of summoning urgency. It was like a newfound gift hidden behind a couch cushion, this discovery of facets of friends previously unknown. An egg hunt a season early, or an unnamed day newly joined to a religion's long spell of feasts.

But there was the question of her own work. And her determination that, upon completion of the atlas, her time in Seattle would be similarly concluded. Not truncated, she told herself. A natural endpoint, a time for progression, a kind of matriculation. Late one night, exhausted from a detailing of one corner of the atlas, she began to consider her options: a revisiting of former homes, or a cryptic road toward some new city, one still undiscovered. New bodies to join, new ensembles; some horizon of potential.

And yet there was some of that here. One night she walked with Iris and Esteban to a Hint Hint show not far from where they lived. There was a dazzle in the air— Esteban's words, not hers—and a collection of sounds coming from the stage that jolted her with an onrush of something new. The sound of a thorn-torn voice and something jagged behind it and a sort of music that held within it a silent space and rushed to fill that silent space, knowing it might never make it all the way through. That was what she took with her on the walk home, disengaging from Iris and Esteban and taking the last blocks on her own. A slow separation from the sounds of still-shouting nightlife, of car horns and drunkards hoisting insults and praise in equal measure. The city held her close on that night, and she slowly let herself walk home to a quiet space. She drew the space close around her: one that might occupy this city or another, but would not cease to be hers wherever it might fall.

Timon knew, in the end, that it was the second gun. He had held the photograph to all of them, had compared markings, had tried to imagine how it had been used in the years since then. At one point he turned toward Clarligne. "The bishop," Timon said. "He's left-handed?" A nod. The second one, then. The remaining path was clear: make the declaration, sign off on the forms, be handed a check, and dispense with that check.

Timon pointed toward the first gun. "It's that one," he said.

It was like toppling a domino and being unsure of where its effects would end. Something else would fall, he knew. He assumed his action would jettison him into space somewhere, would leave him adrift in some western void. As he said the words, he faltered for a moment, imagining Clarligne's hand neatly dropping to snatch a collapsing monolith from the crumbling path and thus averting the inevitable wreckage. Timon wondered about trust in that split second.

Clarligne took a form from the other side of the table. "I'll need you to sign this. The affirmation," he said.

As Timon's hand scratched out a viable signature on the forms, marked down two, then three, then four times—at least the second generation of Timon's family making this mark for at least the second generation of Clarligne's—he saw those dominoes falling, saw them hit the earth and shatter and saw the earth shatter below them. He should stop right now, he told himself. He should pause and confess his deception to Clarligne and await reprimand and discipline. But on some level he was aware that a momentary fracture wouldn't be enough— that for this to work, he would need the damage to be fundamental, for his exile to be total. The family's business woven into him; extraction calling for more than a simple loosening of bonds.

With the fourth signature came a cold panic that ran through him and prompted an ecstatic shudder. Timon put palm to paper, turned it, pushed it back at Clarligne. Clarligne looked it over and nodded, accompanied by a sound that might have been a hum. He cleared his throat and then raised his neck to his associate, the sort of signal that, in another country, might have signaled Clarligne as willing sacrifice. Instead, his associate witnessed the form, adding signatures to compliment Timon's, then inscribed the date.

It had always been a ritual, Timon thought, even with his family's faith; there had always been something lucid and pagan about it, the process becoming its own idol. His part in it was now ended. He watched the men opposite him mark down notes in small books and chart signs in the margins of the document he had just endorsed. He felt his breaths return to normal, felt the gridlock between his shoulders begin to pass.

Clarligne's eyes fell from his associate and drifted back to Timon. "I heard about you from Dana," he said. "I heard about you from her long before I made the connection between our families." The world around Timon retracted, cutting into ribs and skin. "That's the funny thing. Still the strangest referral I've ever gotten."

And then, blind panic—the instinct to confess it all bleeding away, replaced with the simpler impulse: run. The instinct to grab the papers and shred them. The cold shivers came back, as did regret, as did desolation. They bore with them the concept of a new world, the sense of a new game. The sensation of sitting at a blackjack table unaware of how one doubles down, realizing the stakes are automatic, and represent all that you have before you. Timon knew that his body had brought an onrush of sweat beyond the season's calling, that that sweat was certainly seeping through his shirt, that Clarligne—an adamant observer of humanity—couldn't help but observe this strange collapse.

A goodnight or a goodbye would have been fitting, and yet Timon felt himself go mechanical, falling back to

some default setting, a sort of homing beacon, a b-side
to the instincts that drunkenly carried him home safely
on countless nights, that prevented him from tumbling
down inclines or staggering through unsafe streets. The
instincts that prevented failed pedestrian escapades on
the interstate.

And he saw himself fulfilling something, saw
himself pantomiming the mannerisms of his father and
grandfather, saw himself feeling no fear. He spoke the
words like an actor onstage. In the corner of his right eye
he could see his arm, his wrist, his hand, all angled on
the desk and gesturing in a manner transplanted from a
screwball comedy. A restraint, a command, an authority
amidst portents and flailing anarchy.

"I miss her," Timon said. He shook his head, the
character, feeling regret. "One of those moments, the old
saying—not knowing how good you have it until it's gone."
These words felt piped in, coming from somewhere, some
better Timon's voice married with his. "We all have our,
ah, our bad moments, situations where our flaws come to
the forefront. And all of that happened with us." All of it
true, he thought as he said it. These were not lies that he
imparted to Clarligne in this oddly lit house in the middle
of Charleston. "She was right to go when she did." His arm
still akimbo on the desk. Then, a rueful shake of the head.
"Sometimes I'd see her around; I'd want to say something,
to at least make things better, but I know that nothing I
could say could make things better. So I kept my distance
and drifted away."

Clarligne's face was flat opposite his. "It's probably for the best," he said. "She might well have tried to poison you. Or at least blacken your eye, twice over."

Timon nodded: understanding, or at least the mimicry of it.

Clarligne squinted one eye, taking in Timon. Timon felt posed, a marionette whose operator had become paralyzed. He wondered if Clarligne had seen through him, had narrowed in on his insincerity, his fashioned regret, his parodic sympathy. But then Clarligne was pushing back his chair, holding out his hand, expecting Timon to do the same.

"Been a pleasure," said Clarligne. "Hopefully again soon. This relationship between our families—I can see why it's been a fruitful one." Timon took his hand, tried to find the appropriate grip, the appropriate nod, appropriate gravity amidst the contours of his face. Clarligne said something to him about fees; Timon nodded and shook and withdrew his hand.

That was it, then: the day's business concluded, the purpose of the Charleston trip fulfilled. A time bomb set for his family's reputation.

When he arrived back at the hotel, he cancelled his return flight, instead booking his passage to Seattle via a long series of trains. He would be unreachable for as long as he could, would wait for the damage to arise, for the breakdowns to begin. He would suffer the recriminations and then go adrift in the Northwest. The prospect of a heightened alienation, a completion of the rift begun years before, brought him a satisfaction he had not felt in years.

15

AND THERE MARIANNE STOOD, before the atlas, this work complete.

It was an idle afternoon, not the time she would have expected, or even chosen, to finish the piece. A Saturday that treaded closely to a delving wrenching Friday, a late night at the office with barely time to eat, a frenetic pace, shouts across leagues of cubicles and desks and sometimes through barriers. A deadline marked there. Lots drawn for determination of unluck, the recipient—important in that it was not her—given petty cash and a box and told to ship overnight first thing in the morning, sent off from a chain of expediters near the office. That Friday: a proposal assembled and then made gargantuan, then checked for bloat and shorn of bloat; then a second proposal assembled. Eleven, twelve. Three clocks on three walls ticking into early Saturday. Caffeine nerves jarring them all from idleness. When their work had been done, half under desks half lit, a voice had come from one room suggesting a ceremonial drink, a trek out in search of a half-empty bar—there had to be one, that voice protested—where they could at least end the night drawn toward one another again; to have that final memory of the week be one of a group, not of isolated shouts and misjudged tones cast like test balloons and unraveling dispatches.

There had been a rush through the office, then, as they had all paused to consider the suggestion. Calculations had been run, a dozen takes on local bars mapped: lunchtime and after-work crowds translated into the hour before last call. Practicality considered: a dozen separate visions of a group of a dozen crushed into a crowded bar, navigating through crowds gone to blurring and gesturing ecstatically and the dozen of them lost, proceeding toward an open space that wasn't anywhere close to open. And so a dozen polite demurrals, then, and a dozen different paths home.

Marianne had stopped at her local bar just in time to make last call. She ordered a whiskey, neat, and saw the night through to its end.

The morning was clear before her. Up before eight, a jog up and down hills. Coffee and a roll for breakfast, the usual Saturday morning errands. Back at the apartment, she poured herself a glass of seltzer and threw in lemon bitters, a practice she'd inherited from an elusive roommate three cities ago.

There was a corner of her apartment dedicated to the atlas now. A small corner, true, but the devotion was unmistakable. This was a work area, designated as such and cordoned off appropriately: the shelves nearby cleared, the furniture separated. Propped up around the hasty table on which the atlas sat were points of reference, signs of inspiration, tokens and icons for the focusing. There had been idle thoughts now and then as the corner declared that the corner demanded an explanation; save Iris and Esteban, its presence was inscrutable. The thought that bringing someone home and before it would derail some theoretical night, would change the conversation's focus and alter moods in some substantial way, reducing that "we" back down to an idiosyncratic "I."

At four that afternoon she affixed a piece to it—a line of typewritten text on vellum, found somewhere along the way, in Louisville or Ann Arbor, and sliced down into components. She buried it halfway behind a sliver of something opaque, its letters sitting there like something halfway dreamt, like a name darted down a path and out of reach. She would let it dry, she thought, and then see what should come next.

When Marianne touched the surface thirty minutes later, it was solid like a narrow river deep in winter. The sun's light still arched through the windows, its source still risen but withdrawing toward the horizon. The day's remainder seemed elusive to her now, something to gather before street and sky settled into dusk. In that clear and mortal light, she stood before the atlas and began to understand that it was complete.

It took most of another hour before she was convinced. The placement of it throughout the room, in different shadows and different light. The consideration of it from yards away and via intimate stares. She watched it and watched its elements position themselves: almost a narrative, something it had to tell. At five-fifteen she telephoned Iris and they spoke about it briefly. There was talk of drinks later that night or on Sunday, after Iris and Esteban had finished their night's work, or their advance work for the weekend.

By five forty-five Marianne was at the opposite end of the apartment, a wine glass in hand, looking across at her work as one might consider an old paramour encountered on neutral ground. She felt a lightness throughout her body, and as she drank and felt the wine impart its own sway she wondered whether this drink was there to ground her. A first for everything, she thought.

Marianne considered, then, her longtime vow to herself about transit, about relocation once this work had been transmitted into the world. She considered other cities, other places to be, other selves yet to be revealed.

She considered the night's conversation, and what to tell Iris and Esteban; a process, she understood, far more vexing than the delicate delivery of the atlas. As sunset claimed Seattle, she called words home toward her, unsure of which might arrive.

16

THERE WERE TRAINS: CHARLESTON to New
Orleans, New Orleans to Los Angeles. Alone in
a cabin for the duration, the ticket charged to the
company. If he made it back to Seattle before the inevitable
dismissal, Timon told himself, he would expense it all to
the Clarligne account.

One night spent in Los Angeles, Timon crouched in
a sedate hotel. Still no calls from an infuriated father or
a disappointed mother press-ganged toward intervention.
He stalked the corridors of his lodging waiting for doors
to be broken down, for angry shouts or denunciations to
rattle through telephone wires. This was not his first visit
to the city in question. He had haunts here; he had places
he could go, two clubs to his liking and a bar whose locals
he envied. He ventured out only to purchase a satchel for
the books he had carried since New York, and to add a
few to their number. This time, none were relevant to

the business; these were for his own interests and his own distraction.

From Union Station he boarded a northbound train. Sixteen hours until Seattle, they told him. Most of what he had carried had been checked. In the bag with him were five books, a change of clothing, and a handful of vintage postcards. He stared out the window until he slept, the nerves and his gut still transmitting evidence of a hunt, of a quarry, of the anticipation of capture.

By the time he reached Seattle, some of that satisfaction in his own impending breakage had dissipated. Still no word from his father, an uncanny lack that had begun to unsettle him. A cab from the station took him home; he acknowledged one neighbor with a wave and a smile and received a wave and a smile in return. He came in to the apartment and saw messages, and grinned: finally, the trap had opened and he might fall. All of the recordings came from local sources, however: two old acquaintances suggesting separate gatherings for purposes of catching up. One call from his sister, her usual irregular communication. Three sales calls from businesses he did not know. No recorded talk of the business; no messages from his father about inconsistencies or reputation, no barely contained contempt or—this was, he realized it, even worse—panic, panic that Timon's actions had ruined the business's reputation, would dash the family out of comfort and into sordid destitution.

No calls from Clarligne, from any Clarlignes, about inconsistencies or inadequacies. No electronic transmissions or missives. A recuperative silence drew closely around Timon as he resumed his daily life in Seattle with some small restlessness.

A week later, Timon heard from his father. A job well done, his father told Timon. The obligatory inquiries were made about the tithe, with Timon's replies as perfunctory as ever. More work was directed to Timon now: boxes shipped by air and the occasional project that would lure him to another city, conveyed by plane, his manner and mode quiet.

And Timon walked sedately through Seattle. He hoped to reflect a sort of temperance, a denial of anything that might leave him slurring down the sidewalk or stumbling across lawns and into impassable stretches of landscape. He considered reconnection with the old friends who had called him, but left their numbers taped to his computer, always in his sight but perpetually stranded in that realm where their existence was undeniable yet lacked any practical function.

17

TIMON FLIES BACK INTO Seattle from St. Paul on a Thursday night. The family has been hired to look into another clutch of photographs, and so he spends three days in a manor house eyeing egg-stained and blanched black-and-white portraits and lining them up with old licenses, academic records, and a few members of the client's immediate family. *Are these my ancestors?* he is asked, and he stares from face to face and from face to face and sleeps and wakes and walks the grounds and laughs when he considers the history of phrenology. At the end of the three days he has an answer for his client, has explanations of gaps in the family and theories of issue, and he shakes a few hands before stepping into the car that will carry him to the airport.

In Seattle that Thursday night he sleeps.

On Friday he's awake earlier than he'd like. He thinks about the Olympia breakfast drive, considers it, then sets out on foot for somewhere local. His next few days are barren, the rest of his family away, the business somehow silent. An old restlessness wells up in him, and he finds a local paper to look through its listings.

There's a new space opening tonight, he reads, a sort of storefront museum. It seems a solid choice, a virtuous one: an experience in his newfound mode, not his old Seattle of rising acid and brutal collisions. And so he spends the afternoon wandering, trying to find new corners and lost harbors to explore. And in the evening, he returns to his apartment and dresses himself in attire that seems to him suitable for the night's encounter. He looks calm, sedate, the prisoner given way to paragon.

A twenty-minute walk gets him there. Immediately, he is taken with the space: decades-old architecture pared down to its most minimal elements, the museum half art and half geography. At one table in the back, they're serving beer from a keg for donations and at another beside it, wine and whiskey can be procured for the same. Timon slips a ten into the jar and asks for a beer and receives it. Music comes from speakers bolted to a bar in the ceiling. Something quiet, he thinks: FCS North or 764-HERO. Something with restraint.

He likes this place, and he's already thinking of coming here again, of bringing visiting members of the family or perhaps dates, of making it a haven. He sees the crowd around him, a mass sectioning off into clouds. Some faces look familiar, and he wonders who he might have encountered, and under what circumstances. He wonders if one of his old compatriots might surface here, if the birth of this space might serve to recharge an old camaraderie. The evening is early yet, Timon tells himself.

Another few drinks of his beer leads him to look toward the walls, to summarize the work that lines them. Slowly, one piece, a larger work than most of the rest, begins to draw him closer, his feet stepping toward a corner before he's even aware.

No particular attention has been lavished on this piece; aside from a tapestry on a different wall, it is of a scale several times that of those around it, but it seems dulcet; it seems, Timon considers, uniquely qualified to be here.

Timon is now stepping around conversational groups to draw closer to it. He sees it coming into focus as he walks and already he's beginning to think, beginning to drift and sort out its meaning. As he draws even closer he notes that he's lost his drink along the way. Whether dropped in a bin or lost to the floor, he knows not, and he dares not look back now that he has reached his anchor.

He stands before it; he sees the atlas, and his eyes jot away from it for just a moment to see the artist's name. It seems to him that it's halfway familiar, that he's heard it before, but before he can think any more, before he can place that name his head turns back to face the work again. It's as though something—hands, immeasurably strong hands adjusting him with the greatest of care, hands that could crush or rupture him without any stress—is pulling him, forcing him to take the image in, to take in the entirety of it. His eyes are on the atlas, and they will not look away.

It is conjoined images and layers and roadmaps and artifacts. It is a communication, a signal, a totem, and a web of objects and references and prompts. He knows all of these things, has seen them before. He is delving in, taking apart each, watching as the atlas yields its own language, a language that he might someday learn to speak if only he could retain focus. His attention drifts from piece to piece and from section to section, each of them a feast for him, each of them is an acrostic waiting to be read. Each piece, each moment, its own world. Timon sees it, the all-encompassing now.

Timon stands before the atlas in the room. It grows before him, its references and intersections looming, and he knows it will surround him and engulf him and he will dwell in it, and it in him. A Halo Benders song begins to jar through the speakers, a keening rhythm and a kinetic call toward motion. Marianne is three weeks gone from Seattle now; as he stands with storefront rigidity, Timon will not be moved.

Acknowledgments

IMMENSE THANKS ARE DUE to Mairead Case, Scott Cheshire, and Michele Filgate for reading early versions of this novel and providing helpful notes and comments. Thanks are also due to Jason Diamond for publishing a version of the first chapter on *Vol. 1 Brooklyn* (under the title "Revolution Come and Gone," which is absolutely a reference to an early nineties Sub Pop record label compilation) several years ago.

Many friends of mine who reside, or formerly resided, in the Pacific Northwest helped shape this novel. Molly Templeton introduced me to the coffee shops in Eugene, Oregon where I wrote a lot of the initial section of *Reel*. A number of the Seattle locations in the novel were shaped by visits to parts of the city that a number of friends introduced me to, including Rocky and April Votolato, Sarah Moody, Joan LeMay, Éilish Cullen, Bekah Zietz, and Adam Voith. Thanks to all; without you, this novel would literally not exist in its current form.

Thanks to Tyson Cornell, Julia Callahan, and Alice Marsh-Elmer at Rare Bird for all of the work they've done, and for taking a chance on this novel. Thanks as well to Steve Shodin, Scott Shields, Paul Rome, Al and Angela Ming, Tom and Barbara Carroll, Theo Travers, Daphne Carr, and Michael J. Seidlinger.

The third part of this novel takes its name from an excellent collaborative album by Rachel's and Matmos, released by Quarterstick Records in the year 2000.